W9-BFC-361

Brian Landon's other works:

A Grand 'Ol Murder (Doyle Malloy #1)

The Case of the Unnecessary Sequel (Doyle Malloy #2)

A Prairie Homicidal Companion (Doyle Malloy #3)

Why Did Santa Leave a Body? Yuletide Tales of Murder and Mayhem

For Michelle

Unzipping the Parka

by
Brian Landon

WRONG TURN BOOKS

Contents

Introduction

Debbie Does Delano 1

Entwined 16

Bearly Legal 28

Bed and Breakfast and Mabel. 39

Going Down 52

On the Hunt 63

Ballin' at the Mall 77

State of Affairs 91

Untamed 101

A Ski Lift Named Desire 111

Fifty Shades of Grand Marais 121

Acknowledgements

Introduction

The natural reaction to picking up this book and flipping to the introduction would likely be to question "Who is this guy?" "Why did he write this?" Or, perhaps more pointedly, "what's wrong with him?"

All valid questions.

To be honest, writing these stories was a necessary act of expulsion. A few of the stories had been bouncing around in my head for years. In the midst of writing the fourth entry in my mystery series, I found I couldn't move on until the unusual, pervy stories contained herein were out of my head and on paper for public consumption.

The initial spark that ignited the idea for this book came from the late Joan Murphy Pride, a brilliant, funny author who loved to tell crowds at book signings that she once wrote a sex scene, and that Jessie Chandler and I – her trusty writing partners – told her very sternly that she should never write about sex. "They told me I knew nothing about sex," she would say. "And I told them, *'I've had more sex than you've had dinners.'"*

That got me to thinking...what would Midwestern sex scenes look like? Would there be hot dish? Frost bite? My other books contained more innuendo than anything, so this was new territory for me. After trying legitimate attempts at erotica, I realized very quickly that I couldn't take myself too seriously. And honestly, how does any writer of erotica?

I had a lot of fun writing this. Too much, perhaps.

I must provide the standard disclosure that these stories are a work of fiction and any resemblance to anyone living or dead is completely coincidental. In addition, I do not recommend anyone try any of the acts contained within these stories. You might be thinking, *"Wait a minute – isn't this erotica? Maybe I want to try these things?"* Be warned – things to do not work out well for any of the folks in these stories.

Go ahead and draw yourself a bath, light some candles, turn on some polka music, dish up a large bowl of honeycrisp cobbler, and enjoy!

Debbie Does Delano

The snow was coming down in thick, lustrous flakes. Debbie grew dismayed as the crest of snow along the cabin's window sill increased in height. Each hour, she could see less and less of Lake Rebecca from the comfort of the warm, yet frustratingly lonely cabin.

Curt was late. Very late. Normally she wouldn't mind if he took his sweet time on the lake, sitting in his little fish house, drinking beer, pretending like he really cared whether or not he caught any fish. She understood. It was his guy time. No big deal. But this wasn't any other day. This was their anniversary. *Six months*. Debbie had never dated a guy for longer than six months.

Debbie opened her laptop again and decided to focus on her mid-term biology paper. It was due in a couple weeks, and this certainly seemed like the most ideal time to work on it. After all, what else is there to do at the end of February? Well, Curt obviously. *If* he ever got back to the cabin. Debbie shook her head, trying to toss those thoughts out of her mind.

She stared at the blank screen in front of her. It was as white as the snow. *I wonder if Curt's fish house is getting buried?* Debbie thought to herself. *Maybe I should go check on him.*

No, she wasn't going to do that. Curt was a grown man...well, more or less. He was twenty-five and she was twenty-two. A reasonable age difference, she thought. Perhaps he had slightly more life experience by this point. He could definitely take care of himself, at any rate. And she knew herself well enough to know she only wanted to check on him so she could see him. And touch him. And hold him. And then see where things went from there...

Debbie rubbed her eyes. She was getting distracted again. How the heck was she supposed to write an intelligible paper about meiosis when she had Curt on her mind? And speaking of Curt, why would he say he's going to be back to the cabin at five o'clock and then not show up until after eight o'clock? Or maybe even later? FRUSTRATING.

Punctuality was never an issue with the previous guys she'd dated. Of course, they had been nerdy guys. "Collegiate" was probably the more politically correct term, but there was no getting around it – they were nerds. Physics majors. Chemistry majors. One philosophy major – ack, was that a mistake! Curt was the first guy she'd met at the gym rather than at school.

Debbie typed a few words on her screen. "Meiosis: What Is It?"

"Oh, fuck this," said Debbie, closing the laptop. She stood up, walked to the kitchen, and poured herself a cup of coffee with a splash of Irish cream.

"He'll be here soon," she muttered to herself. "He wouldn't keep me waiting on our anniversary. No, definitely not. I just have to be patient."

She walked over to the window and peered outside. There were many fish houses on the lake. Curt's was three houses down on the far right side of the lake. Or was it four houses down? She couldn't remember – she hated ice fishing and had no desire to spend any time cooped up in a tiny room, waiting for something exciting to happen. That was *so* not her.

What would she do when he got back? Would she let him know that she was incredibly pissed off that he had blown off their evening plans of eating dinner together followed by what she assumed would be a steamy night of romance? Or would she forgive him instantly since, after all, she was really excited for said romance?

Debbie took a sip of her coffee. It was hot. Delicious. She blew on it until it cooled off to the point where she could take a sizeable gulp. Due to her small frame, it didn't take much to start feeling a little goofy.

Without putting too much forethought into it, Debbie walked to the door and started putting on her boots. She was done with waiting. She didn't know what she would do when she saw Curt, but she wasn't going to spend one more minute alone in that cabin. She wrapped a scarf around her neck, pulled her parka on tight, zipped it up, and put her wool hat and gloves on.

When she opened the door, the biting chill of the wind surprised her. She momentarily considered stepping back inside, but she really had no such desire.

She stepped outside into the dark, cold abyss. The snow was deep – at least a solid foot of snow had fallen over the course of the day. She could still walk, so it wasn't too much trouble. That much snow really just caused issues when driving on the roads, and they had no intention of going anywhere for the rest of the weekend.

As she trudged through the snow, she pulled the scarf higher up her face. The cold pierced her eyes and made them water. Hopefully Curt was staying warm enough in his fish house. Usually he would bring a small heater to keep him warm. Today was definitely a day to have it going at full blast, she thought.

She walked past one fish house, which was dark and silent. She assumed that many people decided to not come up to the lake due to the massive amounts of snow that were expected in the forecast.

The next house she came across was clearly occupied. The owner seemed to have a number of outdoor holes that had lines going into them. As she was about to pass the house, a door opened so suddenly that she jumped back.

"Oh, hi there," said an older man, maybe in his late forties or early fifties, wearing a red checkered coat and bomber hat. "Lovely day for a stroll, ay?"

"I could do without all the snow," said Debbie, embracing herself.

"Snow is good," said the man. "Keeps everything nice and quiet for the fishies. They won't expect a thing."

"Have you been catching lots of fish?"

"Not a one," said the fisherman. "But they're getting hungry. I can feel it."

"Well, good luck," said Debbie.

"Thank you, dear," he said as he bent down, looking into one of his fish holes. "Nope, still nothin'."

Debbie continued on. She was *pretty* sure the next fish house belonged to Curt, but she wasn't positive. She had never actually seen his fish house, per se, but he had pointed it out to her several times and spoke about it plenty.

The cold was really starting to get to her. She had worn a decent amount of layering, but it's hard to compete with those biting winds. She shuddered.

As she approached the next fish house, she didn't hesitate. She walk right up to the front side and rapped on the door. She was ready for Curt. Despite all waiting, the boredom, the frustration of being alone inside the cabin – it would all dissipate when she could finally put her arms around her man. She wasn't even mad that he had blown her off to keep ice fishing. She loved him. Just being with him was good enough for her.

As she was getting ready to extend her long, slender, increasingly numb arms to wrap around Curt's generously-muscled body, the door opened revealing a portly man with a Green Bay Packers winter hat and a black NASCAR jacket. His face was red – not from the cold, but clearly from one too many Pabst Blue Ribbon's.

"Is ya here to do some fishin'?" he said, hiccupping.

"No, sorry," said Debbie, turning away.

"Ya sure? They ain't biting, but I got some beer in the cooler if it'll help ya any."

"I'll pass," said Debbie.

"Suit yerself," she heard the man say as she walked at a much faster speed despite the cold-induced sluggishness she was starting to feel.

Finally, she approached what *had* to be Curt's fish house. So she didn't do a perfect job of trying to track him down, but still – she was so excited to finally be with him again. Even a little time in a fish house was better than nothing.

As she neared the fish house, what she heard sounded like a motor. A fairly quiet one – not like a chainsaw or a Harley, but a steady buzzing. Almost a growl.

She knocked on the door. "Curt?"

There was no response.

Debbie knocked again. "Curt, are you in there?"

Again, there was no response.

"Curt, I'm coming in!"

She pulled open the door to discover that the motor was, in fact, her boyfriend's drooling, drooping face snoring profusely as he slouched over in his lawn chair.

"CURT!"

"Huh, what," stuttered Curt as he stood up erectly, using the sleeve of his jacket to wipe the drool off of his chin. "What's wrong? Are you okay?"

"Curt, what are you doing?"

Curt looked at Debbie blankly. "I'm ice fishing." He raised his arms as if to say, *See?*

"You were sleeping," said Debbie.

"It's all part of the experience, honey," said Curt, smiling. "What's going on? You're not mad, are you?"

That he would even suggest that she might be mad

suddenly made the anger start to rise in Debbie and she thought of all the ways she could explain how agonizing it is to be waiting for someone, on your anniversary no less, when you had special plans with that certain someone. Or maybe how lonely it is to be in a spacious cabin all by yourself. Or how selfish it is to ignore your girlfriend or choose ice fishing over her wants and needs. Or maybe explain how when you say you're going to be somewhere at five o'clock, then maybe you should make it your beeswax to be there by five o'clock.

Debbie stomped her feet on the wooden floor. "I'm just really —"

"I'm sorry, baby," said Curt, standing up. He opened his arms, ready for an embrace. "I didn't mean to fall asleep. It just happened. I was just so anxious to spend tonight with you, I think I just got overwhelmed. Sometimes excitement will do that to me."

"Yeah?" said Debbie, suddenly at a loss for words.

"Yeah," he said, putting his arms around her. "You're the best girlfriend a guy could possibly ask for. I'm so glad we get to spend this time together this weekend."

"But you were supposed —"

"I love those boots. They look really cute on you."

"Thanks, they're Uggs. But why didn't you —"

"Deb, will you kiss me?"

Debbie felt her knees go weak. "Okay."

Curt pulled her in close, put a hand behind her head, and locked his lips to hers.

Debbie felt the warmth of his kiss. It spread throughout her body like a wave of erotic fire, but with just the smallest touch of moisture from his nose conjugating between their upper lips, like a special snot lip balm.

"That was amazing," said Debbie.

"I'm not done yet," said Curt. He folded the lawn chair and set it again the wall.

"What are you doing?"

Before she realized what was happening, Curt had one arm under her legs and the other under her back, holding her four feet off the ground.

"Whoa, Curt – let's not do this here in a fish –"

But before she could finish her sentence, she was laying on the wooden boards with her head next to an open hole in the ice. Curt kissed her cheeks, her neck, her ears...it was wonderful. And so deliciously *warm*.

Within moments he was tightening his embrace. She could feel pressure building down south. Either that, or she was losing blood flow due to the cold. It was kind of hard to tell.

Curt unzipped her jacket.

"Honey, honey – it's cold. Let's not."

But as he continued to kiss her, Debbie found she had little ability to resist despite the pungent odor coming from the minnow bucket on the other side of her head. He removed her jacket. Although she felt a chill, she didn't refuse when he removed her shirt.

They continued to make out. Debbie became so intoxicated by the whole experience that she barely noticed when Curt removed her pants, as well as his own. It felt like every part of her body was cold, but she clung to the warmth that Curt's body provided. It was an exhilarating experience.

Curt was getting more aggressive, grabbing a hold of Debbie's arms as he thrust her repeatedly. They were pounding against the wood floor. It was loud. Debbie really hoped that the nearby fishermen didn't notice their extra-curricular fishing exploits.

"Curt, maybe you should –" Debbie began to say, until Curt changed his movements ever so slightly, and Debbie was taken by surprise.

"What were you saying?" asked Curt.

"Nevermind," said Debbie. "Just keep...yeah."

Her head was banging against the wood floor, and there was no getting around it–it hurt. But it was such a new and unusual experience that she wasn't about to put an end to it. With every thrust, it was like thunder rumbling through her head.

"Oh my..."

"Yeah?" grinned Curt.

Debbie nodded. "Oh yeah." She was getting close. With every BANG, BANG, BANG against the floor, she got closer to climaxing.

"Curt...I..." THRUST. BANG.

"Yes?" he said, grunting.

"I... love..." THRUST. BANG.

"Uh-huh."

"Love...you." THRUST. BANG. CRASH.

She got there. Curt must have to, because she heard him scream. Funny, normally *she* was the noisy one.

She felt amazing. Almost like she was floating. What an incredible feeling.

"Hold on to me," said Curt.

"I'll never let go of you, sweetie," said Debbie, as she snuggled up next to him.

"Seriously, hold on tight."

As Debbie opened her eyes, she realized that the fish house itself seemed fine, but outside the little window on the upper side of the rear wall, the trees in the horizon were bobbing up and down. Why would the land go up and down like that? Was their cabin okay? Was there an earthquake?

"I don't think we have much time," said Curt. "You might want to put your pants on. Try not to move too quick."

"What? Why?"

He looked at her with an expression that said, "*Really?*"

"Debbie, the ice broke. We might only have seconds before the ice we're on flips upright and sinks."

Suddenly, the combination of the floating sensation, the numbness in her fingers, the stench of the minnows, and the realization of what had happened...it all crept up on her at once. She felt sick.

"Debbie?"

She didn't respond.

"Debbie, now would be a really bad time to get sick. Try to focus."

Debbie nodded. "Okay."

"You're about to get very cold and very wet. You need to hold onto whatever you can. Keep fighting to stay on the surface. Keep getting air. Don't let yourself get tired. Do you understand?"

Debbie had never heard Curt speak like this before.

It was scary how serious he was. It made her realize that she was in a very grave situation.

"But seriously, Debbie – I would suggest putting your pants on NOW."

Debbie reached for her jeans just as water starting pouring in...from the floorboards, from the fishing hole. It seemed like from everywhere. She pulled the jeans onto her body just as the fish house took a mighty lunge forward.

"Oh God," exclaimed Debbie.

"It's happening," said Curt. "Hold onto my hand."

Icy cold water filled up the fish house at a frightening pace. The entire fish house had flipped ninety degrees so that the door was at the top.

"We need to get out the door and try to get onto solid ice," said Curt. "We may have to swim to get there. Are you up for this?"

"What choice do I have?"

"Exactly," said Curt. "Let's have a little swim."

The water was already up to Debbie's waist and was quickly moving upward. She was excited and hopeful when Curt reached up and grabbed a hold of the doorway and pulled himself out of the sinking fish house, but felt a pang of unbearable dread when she thought, "What if he left me here?" and "What if I can't get out?"

But Curt didn't disappoint her. As soon as he pulled himself out of the fish house and was standing on top, he kneeled down and reached through the doorway and grabbed a hold of Debbie's hands.

"Hold onto me tight, okay Debbie?"

"I will," said Debbie, as her cold, numb, slippery hands accidentally lost contact with Curt's. She shrieked as her entire body dropped into the frigid cold water.

"Debbie!" yelled Curt.

Debbie felt the sensation of a hundred knives slashing at her simultaneously. The cold water was unrelenting. It fought her, beat her down. It made her want to give up, even though she knew she couldn't.

She wanted to scream, but she knew that if she did, the freezing water would enter her mouth and invade her lungs. She couldn't let that happen. So instead, she stared at the light above her, framing the silhouette of Curt. He looked like an angel.

She kicked her legs, even though she couldn't feel them anymore. She kept kicking, and as she did, the light became brighter. Closer.

Her face broke through the surface.

"Debbie!" She felt his hands grab a hold of hers. He pulled mightily.

Her body emerged from the water and she held on tightly as he lifted her out of the fish house and onto the side that was now pointing towards the heavens. Debbie was disoriented, but she could tell that they were floating. They were several yards from the edge of the ice.

"What...do...we...do?" Debbie croaked out, surprised that her voice was barely working.

"We need help," said Curt. "We could swim for it, but that's a last resort. I don't want to put your body through that again."

"I can handle it," said Debbie.

"I don't think so," said Curt. "You look like the

blueberry girl from Willy Wonka."

Debbie didn't have a mirror with her, but she was disturbed by Curt's description.

"I see someone," said Curt. "I definitely see someone. Sir! Hey, Sir! Can you help us?"

Debbie looked around, but it took her a few minutes to focus in on the person Curt was yelling to. She recognized him.

"Sir, can you help us?" yelled Curt.

"Goll dang, you broke up the ice something awful!" yelled the man in the NASCAR jacket and the Green Bay Packers winter hat.

"Can you help us?" repeated Curt.

"I ain't swimming out there," said NASCAR man.

"Cell phone?" yelled Curt. "Do you have one?"

"Well, sure I got one," NASCAR man shouted back. "Who do you want me to call?"

A very flustered Curt said, "Oh, I don't know...a psychic hotline. Just call 911. The police. Rescuers. Get them out here!"

"Okay, all right," said NASCAR man.

But as he dialed on his cell phone, it became abundantly clear to Curt that it wasn't going to matter. The fish house was sinking. The water level below them was rising quickly to the point where the water was nipping at their heels of their shoes. They were going to have to swim for it and hope that they can get enough dexterity to climb on top of the ice from the icy waters below.

"We have to swim again, don't we?" asked Debbie.

"I'm afraid so," said Curt. "Are you ready?"

Debbie nodded. They gripped hands.

As they both voluntarily entered the frozen abyss, Curt and Debbie came to the depressing realization that even a few yards seemed like light years away.

As her body hit the water, it felt like jumping into a swimming pool filled with double-edged razor blades. It hurt. Real bad.

"Ahh!" yelled Debbie. "Fuck!"

"Later, Debbie – later!" said Curt. "For now, we have to make it to the edge of the ice sheet."

Although her perception was a bit off, it looked like an entire football field away from Debbie.

"Oh God," said Debbie.

"I know," said Curt. "Do you trust me?"

Debbie nodded. "I do."

"Don't stop swimming," said Curt.

"I'm...so...cold," said Debbie, kicking her legs behind her, but feeling completely void of all energy.

"Just keep going," said Curt, shivering. "Just...keep... going."

As the edge of the ice get closer and closer, Debbie could feel the world around her begin to darken.

"Debbie?"

It didn't seem that late, but for some reason the sun was sinking and the fog was rolling in and the water was becoming comfortably warm.

"Debbie?"

Then everything went silent.

***

When Debbie opened her eyes, she didn't see a tunnel with a bright light. She didn't see a bridge with her loved ones waiting to bring her over. But she did see a red-faced alcoholic with chewing tobacco dripping down his lips onto his black NASCAR jacket.

"Hey, little miss – I'm glad to see you're still alive and kickin'!"

Debbie tried to respond, but her throat hurt something awful. She looked down and realized she was in a hospital gown. A series of tubes, IV's, and electrodes were attached to her.

"You came dang close to leaving this Earth," said NASCAR man. "You're lucky."

Despite the pain in her throat, Debbie tried her best to formulate a word. "Curt."

"Oh, that fella you came in with? He's fine. He's in the next room."

Debbie sighed. *Good. He's okay.*

"I'm just curious," said NASCAR man. "What were y'all doing to cause the ice to break off like that? What, were ya drilling a new hole or something?"

Debbie considered her options for explanations, then decided to go with the most honest one.

"Yeah," she croaked. "It was something like that."

Entwined

"Are you sure we should be doing this?" asked Heather, glancing nervously around the silent museum, the only entrance to the courtyard. It was closed this time of night. Everything was closed in Darwin, Minnesota this time of night.

"Of course we shouldn't be doing this," said Travis. "That's what makes it so exciting."

"But what if we get caught?"

Travis reached for the doorknob that would lead them outside the museum into the courtyard that held the town's pride and joy.

"If we get caught," said Travis, "we'll have one hell of a story to tell our friends."

"We won't need to tell our friends anything if we're all over the news," said Heather, "which I do NOT want to happen."

Travis led her to the center of the courtyard. "You don't need to worry about a thing, sweetheart. The whole town is sleeping. Besides, this was your idea."

Heather shrugged. "Yeah, I guess. I don't know. I just always thought it could be...memorable."

Travis took her hand and pulled her in close. "It will be memorable, babe. I have no doubt of that."

Heather smiled. "Are you ready?"

"Oh, I'm ready!"

"All right then, bad boy," she said seductively. "Then go for it."

Travis gave her a mighty shove, directly into the 12 foot high twine ball – which was, for many years, the biggest ball of twine in the entire world.

Heather grunted, but continued smiling.

Travis pressed his body into hers, her back contouring along the edge of the twine ball. It was heavy – over 17,000 pounds. The ball didn't budge from its location.

Travis pressed his lips to Heather's. She responded in-kind, vigorously kissing him.

"Is this what you were hoping for?" gasped Travis, removing his mouth from Heather's tongue for just long enough to get the words out.

"Almost," she said, "but not quite."

Travis pulled away for a moment. "You want me to complete the fantasy?"

Heather nodded sheepishly.

Travis shrugged. "If you insist." He reached into his jeans pocket and removed a switchblade. "Now, you're sure about this?"

"Just do it."

"You got it."

With one quick, stabbing motion, Travis plunged

the knife into the ball of twine. He cut a couple tough, taut strands of twine. Then he grabbed her left hand and tied it very tightly with a loose strand of twine. Then he took her other hand and tied it with the other loose strand. By the time he was done tying, she was completely and utterly attached to the ball of twine.

"Can you move?" asked Travis.

"Nope," said Heather. "Kiss me."

"Yes ma'am."

"Wait," blurted Heather.

"What is it?"

"Pants."

Travis grinned. "Good idea." He unbuckled her belt, undid the button of her jeans, unzipped the fly, then pulled her pants all the way off. She was left wearing nothing from the waist down other than a skimpy pair of Victoria's Secret underwear. Travis, on the other hand, decided to go the full monty and pulled off his pants and boxer shorts.

"Get over here," said Heather.

Travis nodded and leaned in to kiss Heather. Kissing turned into making out, making out turned into caressing (well, with Travis' hands, anyway), and caressing turned into thrusting.

"Oh God," said Heather.

"I know, right?" said Travis, kissing her along the neck.

"This is crazy," she panted.

"Oh yeah," he muttered as he continued to grind into her.

"Travis, put something on."

"You sure?" he asked, out of breath.

"Yes, do it."

Travis picked up his pair of jeans. He reached into the back pocket and pulled out his wallet. He opened it up and pulled a sealed condom package from the billfold. He leaned against the ball of twine next to Heather, still trying to catch his breath. "This is amazing," he said.

"For sure," said Heather, feeling almost lightheaded from all the excitement.

"I've never done anything like this before," said Travis, leaning down to get a better view of the condom package in the moonlight. "I mean, I've done it before, obviously, but just never –"

Heather began to fell a strange sensation. It was pleasant, but a little scary. Was she fainting? No, but she did feel peculiarly weightless. "Travis?"

Travis was squinting, trying to find the little tab so he could rip open the condom package. "I know, I know – I'm terrible at opening these. It always takes me way too –" Then Travis paused. Something struck him as odd. "Heather?" He looked over, but she wasn't there. "Heather, where did you go?"

"TRAVIS!

Travis looked up. "What the hell?" He was surprised to see that his girlfriend, whose feet were previously on the ground, were now several feet off the ground. The giant ball of twine had begun, albeit slowly, to roll away and unravel. Heather appeared to be very aware of this, and not pleased.

"Travis, for God's sake, get me down from here!"

"I will, I will — hold on," said Travis, still trying to figure out the condom package.

"Seriously, Travis — if this rolls all the way around, I'll be crushed. It weighs like eight tons. STOP THIS THING!"

Heather could see as she looked down at Travis that he had turned pale. Clearly he finally understood the gravity of the situation. "Keep your head together, Travis. Try pulling on my legs."

Travis nodded. He firmly grabbed her legs and pulled down, but was shocked by the force of the ball pulling her the other direction. She was high enough on the ball now where Travis could feel his own feet lifting off the ground as he held onto hers.

"It's not working," he said. "It's...just too big. Too heavy."

"DO SOMETHING," she said, panic starting to set in.

Travis closed his eyes for a moment.

"What are you doing!?" yelled Heather.

"I'm thinking. I think...yes. I have an idea." Travis ran out of Heather's peripheral vision.

"Travis?"

She didn't hear a response.

"TRAVIS?"

"I'm back," she heard him say. She relaxed. For a second, anyway. She heard a lot of rustling from behind her.

"What are you doing?" she asked.

"I found some stuff in the gift shop," said Travis.

"You went SHOPPING?" yelled Heather, who was

almost directly on top of the twine ball.

"No, but I think this might work. Hold on."

Heather heard grunting, following by a crash and a ding.

"Please tell me what you're doing," said Heather.

"I grabbed the cash register and put it in the twine ball's path. It should stop it," he said.

"I really don't think that's going to be strong enough to —" Heather began to say, as a screeching, snapping, crunching sound erupted from beneath the twine ball.

"I think you're right," said Travis.

Travis was fighting the rising tide of fear in his belly. He tried to push against the ball as it rolled towards him, but it was just too strong. He needed to think of something else. But he became concerned when Heather went several seconds without yelling at him.

"Heather? Are you okay?"

He heard a snort and a whimper. She was crying.

"I don't want to die on a twine ball, Travis. I just don't."

"You're not going to die, Heather! Just listen to me for a minute. You're about to be upside down. Because your feet aren't tied down, you're going to flip over. It's probably going to hurt like a bitch on your wrists, arms, and shoulders. But I'm going to try to hold up your lower half so it won't be quite as dramatic."

"Okay," she said. "But that still doesn't get me off this thing. I'll still be crushed."

"No you won't," he said. "As soon as you're close enough to the ground again, I'll cut your wrists free with my knife."

"You won't have much time," said Heather. "Especially because – OH SHIT."

Just as Travis had predicted, as Heather's head approached the vertical midpoint of the twine ball, the lower half of her body, which was currently above her head, flipped over from gravity.

"Fuck that hurt," she said.

Travis was pulling her legs back. "Just keep your feet away from the bottom. I don't want your feet crushed."

"Okay, yeah," she said. "Cut me down."

"I'm doing it right now," said Travis, reaching up with the knife in his hand.

"Cut me down, cut me down, cut me down, cut me down..."

"Don't panic, baby – I got this."

And he did. Heather looked up and watched one of Travis' strong arms slice and hack at the twine as he continued to hold her with his other arm.

As Heather's feet touched the ground, but her wrists still firmly attached to the twine ball, she felt a sudden burst of terror.

"Faster, Travis. You need to go much, much faster."

"One down, one to go," said Travis.

He was right. Suddenly she had full control of her right hand again. It was freed from its temporary slavery to the twine ball.

"Other one, other one," she said.

"Yes ma'am," he said, working away at her other wrist.

Her attached wrist was now at the height of Travis'

midriff. With one arm free, she was able to maneuver her body a little further away from the twine ball, but she was still far too close for comfort.

"This was a bad idea," said Heather.

"What do you mean? I almost have you freed. You'll be fine," said Travis.

"No, I mean this whole thing. It was stupid."

"Don't be ridiculous," said Travis. "It was a great idea. There was just a little factor that we hadn't considered."

"The fact that balls roll?"

Travis briefly paused. "Yeah."

"No more talking, just cutting. Get me off of here."

"Just about done."

"Thanks for getting me out of this mess," said Heather

"Well, I'm not done yet," he said. "But I wasn't going to let you be killed by a twine ball. I'm far too good of a boyfriend for that."

"I appreciate it," she said.

"And you're officially free," said Travis, cutting through the final tiny strand.

Heather fell to the ground, then scrambled to get as far away from the ball as possible. She lied on her back, staring at the sky, thanking her lucky stars that she was still alive. Travis curled up beside her. He rested his head on her chest.

"Well, this is romantic, isn't it?"

It was just absurd enough to make her laugh.

"What a disaster," said Heather, still laughing.

"You think that's a disaster? Wait until that twine

ball reaches the hill," said Travis. "That's the highway down there."

"Oh shit," said Heather.

"I know."

"Should we do something?" asked Heather.

"I can't stop it," said Travis. "But I suppose we could call the police."

Heather nodded.

"Maybe we should get dressed first," said Travis."Since the police will be coming."

"That's a good idea," said Heather.

As Travis stood up and searched for his cell phone, Heather stood up and searched for her pants. She passed the crushed cash register. Change and bills were scattered about the ground. She briefly considered snatching a little cash for her troubles, but decided that sending the twine ball through town would cause enough damage. The twine ball people were going to need the money more than her.

"Hi. Yes, I wanted to report a umm...emergency situation? The twine ball is on the loose."

Heather found her pants and began putting them on as Travis continued to talk on the phone.

"No, this isn't a prank. It's just about to reach a hill and...yup, there it goes. It's going towards the highway."

Heather buttoned her pants button and zipped up the zipper.

"Seriously, you better send some cars. That fucking thing is heavy."

Travis hung up.

"Do you think they'll actually send the cops to stop the ball?"

Travis shrugged. "It's hard to say. The lady on the phone had a difficult time believing me."

Heather put her arms around Travis.

"You saved my life. Thank you. I love you."

Travis smiled. "I love you, too." Then, Travis looked as though he had just remembered something of great importance.

"What is it?"

Travis pulled out his cell phone again.

"Who are you going to –"

"Not calling anyone," said Travis. "Taking a photo."

"I don't really want to memorialize this, Travis."

"Not of us. The twine ball! I bet the twine ball museum will pay tons for a photograph of the twine ball heading down the road."

"Sure, except for one really important detail, Travis."

"What's that?"

"It's not just rolling. It's unraveling. If that keeps going down the highway, eventually there won't be a twine ball."

Travis swallowed. "Will we be in trouble?"

"Since we sent the twine ball on its merry way, I'd say we'd be in pretty big trouble."

"Shit," said Travis. "What do I do?"

"It doesn't look like it's going that fast," said Heather. "Go get your car."

"You...you serious?"

"Of course," said Heather, putting hands on Travis'

shoulders. "Go stop that twine ball."

Travis nodded. "Okay."

Within seconds, Travis had sprinted through the twine ball museum, into the parking lot, and hopped in his 2007 Toyota Matrix. He turned the engine, put the car in gear, and peeled out of the lot, around the bend, and down the county highway where the giant twine ball was slowly but surely rolling and unraveling. It reminded Travis of *Raiders of the Lost Ark*.

As Travis approached and then began driving alongside the twine ball, he realized he had no solid plan, other than using his car to stop the twine ball in its tracks.

"Shit," said Travis. Granted, he didn't have the best automobile in the world, but he didn't fancy having it crushed underneath an oversized tourist attraction.

But there was no other choice.

Travis took a sharp right, planting the passenger side of his vehicle directly within the path of the twine ball.

Although he knew his car would be damaged, he severely underestimated by how much. The twine ball seemed to engulf the passenger side of his car, so much so that Travis threw open the driver's side door and dove away from the crushed vehicle.

The twine ball had stopped, lodged in the interior of Travis' Toyota.

Travis stepped away and viewed the scene. He had to admire the absurdity of the whole situation. There was really only one thing left he could do at this point. He just wasn't sure if it would work.

He walked back to his car, reached into the center console, and pressed a button.

A voice squeaked out of the speaker – it was heavily distorted from the damage, but Travis could still make it out.

"On-Star – how may I help you?"

This was Travis' first time using the automobile rescue service, and it was a doozy.

"You won't believe what just happened to me."

Bearly Legal

"Steph, will you help me pitch the tent?"

"I'd rather pitch a condo. Seriously, why are we out here?"

Steph was excited to be spending the weekend with her fiancé Scott, but she was not looking forward to spending said weekend in the wilderness of Nisswa, Minnesota. She hadn't been camping since she was a little girl, and even then she'd had her mom pick her up when she realized there was simply no escaping the numerous bugs of all shapes and sizes.

"It's camping," said Scott. "It's fun."

"Do you really believe that?"

Scott shrugged. "Not necessarily. But it's probably healthier than going to the bar every weekend. It'll be something different."

She had to admit, he had a point. They had been discussing for months how they needed to do something to switch up their routine. But Scott never struck her as the outdoorsy type.

Scott was pulling metal rods out of a long canvas bag. "Seriously, can you help me with this?"

"Is it super heavy or something?"

"No," said Scott. "I've just never put one of these things together. My dad said it was pretty easy when he let me borrow this, but I didn't exactly have him go through the step-by-step instructions."

"Oh, I see."

Scott paused. "Is something wrong?"

"No, I just...I assumed you'd done this before."

"I have," said Scott. "I mean, I was probably ten years old, but I remember it pretty well."

"Except for the 'setting up the tent' part of it?"

"I didn't do that," said Scott. "The scout master was in charge of that."

"Oh," said Steph, resigning herself to the fact that it could be an even less fun weekend than she had thought.

"Just help me pull the rest of the tent out of this bag..."

"Wait, are you sure we should set up the tent right here?"

Scott looked around the area where they were standing. There was a smattering of trees and bushes, and they were just a short distance from a small creek that ran north towards the highway.

"I think this is fine," said Scott.

"I don't like how open this is here," said Steph. "Let's go back aways and set up near those raspberry bushes. I'll feel less exposed then."

Scott raised his eyebrows. "Exposed? Are you planning on being one with nature this weekend?"

Steph smiled. "I'm not opposed to the idea of getting a little wild in the wilderness, but I just want to feel like we're somewhat secluded. That's all."

"I get it," said Scott. "Alright, back by the raspberry bushes we'll go. Grab the cooler and your bag. I'll lug the tent over there."

"Wait a minute," said Steph. "Don't raspberry bushes attract, like, bees or something?"

"I don't see any bees around right now," said Scott. "But if there are, do you really care that much?"

"I guess not. You're right."

***

After a few hours of arguing while attempting to erect the tent, the sun was beginning to set. The tent was put together...for the most part. Steph wasn't thrilled that some of the metal rods that were supposed to be the framework for their tent were instead sticking out in random places. Yet the whole thing still seemed relatively tent-like. It would be good enough for the weekend.

"Are you hungry?" asked Scott.

"I'm not starving, but I could eat."

Scott gestured to the cooler. "Go ahead and pull out the hot dogs. I'll get a campfire going."

"Have you ever gotten a campfire going yourself?" asked Steph, removing the lid from the white Styrofoam cooler.

"I have a can of kerosene and a lighter – how hard could it be?"

Steph shrugged. "Wow, these are different," she said as she pulled a long chain of attached wieners out of the cooler.

"Old fashioned skin-on wieners," said Scott. "Nothing but the best."

"But there's no way we can eat all of these," said Steph.

"I know, I over-did things a bit. Why don't you just detach three or four of them, then just hang the rest of them up on our tent."

"On our tent?"

"Sure," said Scott. "We have a few extra rods sticking out. Might as well put them to use, right?"

"Why not," said Steph, hanging the long chain of hotdogs on a silver metal rod that stuck out six inches beyond the front flap of the tent.

"I'm going to get some sticks for the fire," said Scott, heading away from their campsite. "You know, Steph? This might just be the best weekend ever."

***

After successfully igniting a campfire that, to Steph's relief, did not threaten to burn down the entire forest, Scott and Steph proceeded to cook hot dogs and drink beer underneath the darkening sky.

"You can almost see the stars now," said Scott, taking a bite of his hot dog.

"I know – it's actually rather beautiful up here. This just about makes all the bugs and tent set-up and lack of bathrooms worthwhile."

Scott smiled. "I knew you'd come around."

Steph grabbed Scott's knee and gave him a kiss on the cheek. "This was a good idea, Scott. I love you."

"I love you, too," said Scott.

Steph was about to lean in for another kiss when Scott blurted, "Hey, do you know how to catch a bear?"

"What?"

"This is something my grandfather told me a long time ago. How to catch a bear."

"No, I have no idea," said Steph, playing along. "How do you catch a bear?"

Scott picked up a stick and pushed over a fiery log in the campfire. "The first thing you do is dig out a hole in the ground. Then you take all the ashes from your campfire – just like our campfire here – then put it in the hole in the ground. Then you open a can of peas and sprinkle peas along the rim of the hole. "

Scott became silent.

"...and?" asked Steph.

"Hmm? Oh, right. So when a bear goes to take a pea, you kick him in the ash-hole."

It was Steph's turn to be silent.

"I said, 'you kick him in the ash-hole.' Get it?"

Steph stretched her arms into the air. "Well, it's getting pretty late. Might head into the tent."

"You're mean," said Scott.

Steph grinned. "Yeah, a little bit."

"I'll join you," said Scott.

"Umm, shouldn't you take care of a little something first?" asked Steph, gesturing to the blazing fire that they'd just been sitting by.

"Right," said Scott. "I suppose I shouldn't burn Northern Minnesota to the ground."

"Good idea," said Steph.

***

Steph had already changed into her pajamas and crawled into her sleeping bag when Scott entered the tent, a dangling wiener slapping him in the face as he did so. "I should probably put those back in the cooler," he said, but instead headed directly to Steph's sleeping bag.

"What are you up to?" asked Steph seductively.

"Thought I'd spend a little quality time with you."

"That sounds good to me," she said, unzipping her sleeping bag to let Scott in.

"Hold on – I need to grab something."

Steph was confused. Now that she was on the pill, they had stopped using condoms.

"What are you getting?"

"Well," said Scott, digging into his duffel bag, "since we're on a camping adventure, I brought a little something to enhance the experience."

Steph was apprehensive, but also a little excited. "And what did you bring?"

Scott's hand emerged from his duffel bag with a small transparent bottle of golden liquid.

"What is that?" asked Steph.

"Honey," said Scott. "You'd mentioned a few times about adding some food play into our sexual shenanigans. I figured this would be a good opportunity."

"But...out here? Are you sure?"

"Of course, why not?" asked Scott. "If we get a little sticky, we'll just use a little canteen water to clean up."

It made sense to Steph. "Okay – let's do it."

Scott kissed Steph on the lips. "I'm thrilled that we have this weekend together. "

"Me too."

Scott lifted Steph's pajama shirt, exposing her midriff. Scott poured a fair amount of honey all around her navel.

"Oh, that feels nice," said Steph. "Is my big bear hungry?"

"Mmm," said Scott. "You know it."

The twenty minutes that followed was just as sweet as Scott had imagined.

***

Steph awoke at 2:30am to a full bladder that required immediate relief. After unzipping the sleeping bag that she had been sharing with Scott, she discovered that she was sticky. Very sticky. Everywhere.

"Eww," said Steph, quietly enough so she wouldn't wake up Scott.

She dug in her duffel bag for a long t-shirt that she could throw on and be somewhat decent outside the tent. She realized she was amongst nature, but she didn't find it necessary to show off all her happy bits to the local owl population.

She left the tent and attempted to scout out a reasonable place with which to relieve herself. She decided to walk behind the tent and several yards down towards the end of the row of raspberry bushes. It was tucked away and provided as much privacy as the great outdoors can give.

As she squatted down and became one with nature, she heard a bizarre rustling noise. It was nearby, couldn't be further than a couple yards.

"Hello?" she said, realizing quickly that her voice sounded incredibly loud in such a quiet environment.

The rustling sound stopped. The only noise was the flow of her urine stream, which harmonized majestically with the creek behind the raspberry bushes.

As Steph stood up, she heard a peculiar noise. It was like rapid, rushing air. It sort of reminded her of when her childhood dog Sasha would sniff her face and...

Oh. Crap.

The realization that she was still coated in honey struck her as a very, very bad situation. She didn't know which savage animal was on the other side of the raspberry bush, but she was certain that, whatever it was, probably wouldn't mind having a honey-marinated meal.

The sniffing noise stopped. It was quiet. Steph breathed a sigh of relief.

Then the rustling started. The creature was shaking the bush. Its head was likely buried in the bush, eating as many raspberries as it could find.

Steph decided it might be a good idea to get back to the tent. She took a step back, and then another. But then her foot slipped, sending her body to the ground, landing in...to her disgust, her own urine.

She would have spent more time stewing about how gross her situation had become, but she heard footsteps...more like pounding on the ground, really...and she took off running.

She looked behind her. She could see it now. It wasn't anything like her childhood pup Sasha; no, this was much bigger. It was a black bear.

When she got to the tent, she stood on the other side of it, hoping she lost the bear.

"Scott," Steph said in a low tone, hoping to wake up Scott, but not attract the bear.

But it didn't matter. The bear had found her. As it approached, still sniffing the air and likely picking up the scent of honey and urine, Steph's jaw nearly dropped as the bear reared up on its hind legs. The bear was a giant.

Without knowing what to do, Steph did the only thing that came to mind. She reached out and grabbed a hold of the chain of wieners that were conveniently hanging from the front of the tent. She tore off the wieners one by one and threw them at the bear.

Steph was pleased to see that the bear was eating the hog dogs. Heck, he really seemed to like them! The only problem was that there were about ten of them, and she had just thrown all of them at the bear. They were gone. The bear still licking his chops. He was hungry.

With her body covered in honey and her hands covered in wiener juice, Steph did the only thing left at her disposal. She ran as fast as she could.

She could hear the bear follow. She didn't need to look – she knew it was there. She also knew that it was only a matter of seconds before it caught up to her and ate her.

But she only needed a few seconds. As soon as she

ran past the last of the raspberry bushes, she could see the creek. It wasn't the ideal way to leave the campsite – she would have preferred using their vehicle – but it was better than being eaten.

She turned her head. The bear was only a few paces behind her. That gave her just enough fear and adrenaline to dash towards the creek and dive in.

As her body entered the cold water, she was thrilled to have an advantage over the bear. She was an excellent swimmer and felt confident in her abilities. On the other hand, however, the water was *really fucking cold.*

She could see behind her that the bear had entered the water as well, but he was far away now, getting smaller and smaller as the current and her own momentum carried her along.

She knew which way she was headed. She knew eventually there would be a bridge and a highway. She also knew she'd be mostly naked waiting for some random stranger to pick her up and bring her to safety.

Maybe she should have given the bear another shot.

***

Scott awoke with arms stretched out to the sky. He couldn't remember the last time he had slept in the outdoors, but by golly he felt good!

Scott looked around. "Steph?"

He didn't hear a response.

"Honey?"

Still nothing.

Scott shrugged his shoulders, flipped onto his side, and shut his eyes.

Camping is awesome, he thought.

Bed and Breakfast and Mabel

A trip to Two Harbors for a honeymoon wasn't exactly the most extravagant getaway, nor was it the warmest. But for Kristy and Rob, it was the best they could do on a limited budget. Besides, it really wasn't about the place, anyway. All that mattered was that they were spending this special time together after devoting themselves to each other for the rest of their lives.

Someplace tropical would have been nicer, thought Rob, as he stepped foot into "Grandma Mabel's Bed and Breakfast."

The house was old – there was no getting around that. The floorboards creaked as they stepped foot into the foyer. It smelled musty. It was hard to tell if that was because moisture from nearby Lake Superior had seeped into the foundation of the home over the years or if it had simply taken on that "old person smell." Rob had grown up with his grandparents, so he knew that smell well. It was comforting. But it also wasn't Jamaica.

"I like this place," said Kristy. "It's charming."

"Mmm," agreed Rob half-heartedly.

"Are you excited for a full week away from work? Completely alone? With me?"

Rob looked at his blushing bride's slender figure. "Absolutely," he said. "I mean, I wouldn't say I'm totally sold on this place yet, but I love being with you."

"Aww," said Kristy, grabbing Rob's hand. They walked towards a small desk in the corner of the foyer. There was a gold desk bell, just like in old fashioned hotels.

"Want to ring it?" asked Kristy.

Rob shrugged. "Sure."

He slammed his hand on the bell, causing a loud *DING!* Within moments, an older woman – perhaps in her seventies – descended the staircase on the opposite side of the foyer and approached the small desk near Rob and Kristy.

"Can I help you?" the old woman asked.

"Yeah, we're the Peterson's," said Kristy.

"Okay?" said the old woman, confused.

"We have a reservation," added Rob. "We're here on our honeymoon."

The old woman's face lit up. "Oh, how wonderful! When did you get married?"

"Yesterday," said Kristy. "Now that we're done with the ceremony and being around our families constantly, we're finally able to be alone."

"Thank God!" said Rob. "I mean, I love her family and everything, but it's definitely time to enjoy our marriage."

"That is just lovely," said the old woman. "My name

is Mabel. My husband left me this house when he passed away, and it was far too big for just me, so I turned it into a bed and breakfast. I think you'll enjoy it here. I will try my best to take care of all your needs."

"That's great," said Kristy. "You have a beautiful home."

"Thank you, dear. What did you say your name was?"

"Kristy. Kristy Peterson."

"Oh, right. And what can I do for you, Kristy?"

Kristy looked apprehensively at Rob. "We had a reservation?"

"Oh, yes of course," said Mabel. "Let me look at my book, here. I'm nothing without my book."

Mabel pulled a leather ledger from the drawer of the desk. She flipped it open and located their names.

"Rob and Kristy Peterson, yes, right here," said Mabel. "I have you booked in Room 3 – the Tranquility Room. I think you'll enjoy it."

"I'm sure we will," said Kristy.

Mabel studied the ledger. "There are only two other couples staying this weekend, so it should be nice and quiet for you. What brings you to my bed and breakfast?"

Rob coughed. "We're on our honeymoon?"

"Oh, how lovely," said Mabel. "When did you get marr –"

"I'm sorry to interrupt, Mabel," said Rob. "Any chance you could show us the Tranquility Room?"

"Most certainly," said Mabel. "There I go, chatting up a storm again. Sometimes I just lose track of myself.

Ever have that feeling?"

"Probably not quite like you," said Rob. Kristy slapped him and frowned. Rob shrugged.

"I swear, the older I get the harder it is to keep track of everything. I guess that's why most folks eventually retire, right? Not me. I'd be far too bored," said Mabel.

"I totally understand," said Kristy. "I would get bored too."

"Bored doing what?" asked Mabel.

"Umm...being retired," said Kristy.

"You can't be retired at your age," said Mabel. "You don't look a day over twenty-five."

"No, I didn't mean – well, thank you of course, but what I meant..." Kristy paused when Rob elbowed her in the side. "Can you show us our room? The Tranquility Room?"

"Yes, right this way, please," said Mabel, escorting them up the staircase. "You know, my husband left this house for me after he passed away."

"You don't say," said Rob. Kristy delivered another elbow to his ribs.

"I turned the four bedrooms on the second floor into guest rooms," continued Mabel. "Over there is the Blue Room, down the hall is the Serenity Room, at the opposite end is the Relaxation Room, and here is the Tranquility Room. Now...which room did I have you in again?"

"The Tranquility Room," said Kristy.

"Oh, right. I swear, my mind has taken a vacation," said Mabel apologetically.

"No worries at all," said Kristy. "We're just

happy to be here."

"Wonderful," said Mabel. She handed Kristy a door key. "I'll have some light snacks available in the living room this evening. Otherwise, breakfast will be served at 8:00 a.m. If you need anything at all, just let me know."

"Thank you so much," said Kristy.

"Of course, dear. You kids have fun."

"We will," said Rob.

Kristy looked at him and shook her head playfully.

***

The Tranquility Room, to Kristy's surprise, was unusually noisy. The floorboards squeaked underneath her feet. The bed screeched when she sat down on it. The ships outside were sounding their horns as they entered the harbor.

"This is nice," said Kristy, despite the fact that she was underwhelmed.

"It's okay," said Rob. "It's older than I was expecting."

"I like the nautical theme," said Kristy, observing the bedspread with the image of an anchor stitched into it. Artwork of ships and sailboats adorned the walls.

"Not bad," said Rob. "But honestly, I don't care where we stay. I have been dying to finally be alone with you, babe. We're finally married and we finally have some private time together."

"Oh, you think something is going to happen?"

"A guy can wish, can't he?"

Kristy smiled. "You won't be disappointed."

"Oh yeah?" said Rob, sitting down next to Kristy on the bed.

"Yeah," said Kristy, pressing her lips to Rob's.

They were suddenly interrupted by a knocking on their door.

"Come in," said Kristy.

Rob looked perturbed by the interruption, but Kristy was pleased to see the sweet old lady from downstairs again. Mabel was carrying a small pile of blankets.

"I'm sorry to bother you," said Mabel, "but I was dreadfully afraid that I didn't leave enough blankets for you to keep warm tonight."

"That's so thoughtful," said Kristy. "Thank you."

Rob, still looking bothered, said, "Yeah, thanks."

"You're welcome," said Mabel, setting the blankets on the bed beside them. "If there's anything else you need tonight, please let me know."

"Of course," said Kristy.

"Have a lovely night," said Mabel, closing the door behind her.

Kristy turned her attention to Rob. He looked relieved that Mabel was gone.

"Okay, so where were we?" asked Kristy.

Rob put his left arm around Kristy's shoulder and brushed his right hand through her hair. He pulled her in tight for a kiss.

"That's what I was hoping for," said Kristy.

Rob grinned. "It gets better from here." He grabbed the pile of blankets that Mabel had left for them and flung them on the floor. Then he turned to Kristy and gently pushed against her chest until she was laying flat on the bed. He pulled himself on top of her.

A sudden, loud knocking disturbed the romance once again.

"Come in," said Kristy, pushing Rob off of her and into a sitting position.

"Sorry to bother you kids," said Mabel, "but it's a bit drafty in this old house and I thought you could use some extra blankets to get through the night."

Kristy saw Mabel's attention drift to the pile of blankets on the floor next to the bed.

"Well, I see you already helped yourself to the linen closet," said Mabel. "That's a little unexpected, but if you're chilly, then I understand."

"Thank you, Mabel," said Kristy. "We really appreciate it."

"Yeah, right," muttered Rob.

Mabel gave him a disapproving look, which led to Kristy giving him a disapproving look.

Rob looked at both of them and said, "Listen, I'm sorry. I was really hoping to have some private time with my new wife tonight. I don't mean to be rude."

"Oh, of course," said Mabel, handing Kristy the additional pile of blankets. "Dearie me, where are my manners? I'll let you kids be."

"Thank you," said Rob.

Mabel made a hasty exit.

"That was a little mean," said Kristy. "She's just trying to be nice."

"I know," said Rob. "It's just frustrating. That's all."

Kristy still looked hesitant.

"I'm sorry. Let's not let this ruin our weekend," said

Rob, putting his hand on her leg.

Kristy conceded. "Okay, you're right. It's not a big deal."

Rob smiled. "Good."

Kristy grabbed the bottom of Rob's shirt. She lifted it up and pulled it over Rob's head.

"What are you doing?" asked Rob.

"Making up for lost time," said Kristy.

She pushed her hand against Rob's bare chest, forcing him to lay down. She kissed him repeatedly from neck to belly button.

"That's great," said Rob. "Keep doing th—"

Suddenly, the door opened.

"Whoa, whoa, whoa," said Rob, as he sat up. He looked over at Kristy. Even she looked flustered this time.

"What in the name of William A. Irvin are you kids doing in my Tranquility Room?"

Rob and Kristy glanced at each other with befuddled expressions.

"We rented it for the night?" said Rob, hoping his response would be acceptable.

Kristy nodded enthusiastically.

"Oh, you did? Oh, my – I'm sorry. I must have forgotten," said Mabel, lowering her head. "I see you've helped yourself to my linen closet." She stared at the pile of blankets on the floor.

"You gave –" Rob began to say, until he was elbowed in the ribs by Kristy. "Ow."

"We were cold, so we got them. Sorry about that – I hope we weren't too imposing."

"Oh, no – of course not, dear. I'm glad you'll be warm tonight," said Mabel. "Well, I'll get out of your hair now. You kids have a good night."

"Thank you," said Kristy.

"Hmmph," muttered Rob.

As Mabel exited the room and closed the door behind her, Rob ran to the door and frantically inserted and slid the chain lock.

"What are you doing?" asked Kristy.

"No more interruptions," said Rob. "I can't take it."

"Sweetie, sit down," she said, patting the bed beside her.

Rob sighed. He walked back to the bed and sat down.

"You know she's just a sweet old lady with Alzheimer's, right? She's not trying to ruin your night."

"That doesn't change the fact that it's happening," said Rob.

"It's a long night," said Kristy. "We have plenty of time."

"It definitely feels like a long night," said Rob. "Christ almighty."

"Don't let it get to you like that. I don't want to spend our honeymoon complaining and arguing."

"I'm not arguing," said Rob. "I think we're both in agreement that getting interrupted every time we dare be intimate is really, really annoying."

Kristy was silent for a moment. "Let's just lay down and forget any of that just happened. Okay?"

Rob still looked irritated but gave in. "Okay."

Kristy kissed him. It was good. It was enough to

make him relax and forget what was bothering him in the first place. But as time ticked by and their kisses, caresses, and motions became increasingly intimate, Rob found himself glancing repeatedly at the door.

"What?" asked Kristy.

"Nothing."

"Just pay attention to this," said Kristy as she lifted her shirt above her head.

"Sounds good to me," said Rob, once again forgetting what had been irritating him. He reached for the front of her jeans, unbuttoning and unzipping them. He began pulling them down...

A loud rapping on the bedroom door caused Kristy and Rob to flinch and jump back from each other. Kristy tumbled off the bed, hitting her head on the nightstand.

"Ow," said Kristy, rubbing her forehead.

"Shit," said Rob. "Are you okay?"

"Who's in there?" yelled Mabel from outside the room.

"YOUR TENANTS!" screamed Rob. "WE PAID TO BE HERE. THIS IS OUR ROOM. JUST GO AWAY."

Silence followed. The only sound was of Rob and Kristy's breathing. The silence became uncomfortable.

"Are you okay?" asked Rob.

"No," said Kristy. "Let's just go to bed."

"Whoa, wait – but this is our honeymoon," said Rob.

"It's not working," said Kristy.

"What do you mean –"

"We'll do another honeymoon. We can go

somewhere else. Let's just go to sleep. I'm done."

"Shit," said Rob. "Should we take a look at your forehead?"

"It's fine. Just turn off the light."

"Okay."

***

Kristy woke up in the middle of the night. Not for any particular reason. She just felt a little restless. She thought about what she'd said to Rob, how she'd shot down any further chance of a decent honeymoon during their stay at the bed and breakfast. She knew it wasn't anyone's fault, but the circumstances just weren't right. But she felt bad for Rob. He deserved better.

Rob was sleeping beside her, but she could tell he was sleeping lightly. Normally he snored loudly when he was in deep sleep. She rubbed his back.

"Mmm?" he asked."What's up?"

"Are you awake?" asked Kristy.

"Now I am," said Rob."What's going on?"

"It's been hours since Mabel was here last. I'm sure she's asleep. I know this hasn't gone the best – but, do you still want to try?"

"Are you suggesting what I think you're suggesting?" asked Rob.

"Yeah."

"Okay, I'm on board," said Rob.

"Check the hallway," said Kristy. "Make sure she's asleep."

"Sure," said Rob, pulling himself out of bed. He

went to the door, unlocked it, and opened the door.

"All clear?" asked Kristy.

"Oh yeah," said Rob."It's pitch black out there."

"Excellent," said Kristy."Get over here."

Rob closed the door and hurried back to the bed. He wasn't going to waste a single minute this time. He tore her shirt off. She pulled his pants off. Within mere moments they were tangled up in each other, moving and thrusting, panting and moaning.

Rob reached a moment of such intensity that he thought he was seeing lights flash before his eyes. When he opened his eyes and focused, he realized that he was seeing lights. And their door was open.

"Ahhh!" yelled Rob.

"What?" asked Kristy, not realizing what was happening.

"Sorry to interrupt," said Mabel. "I was just so excited to realize that I have guests in our Tranquility Room! Is this a bad time?"

"YES!" yelled Rob.

Kristy, who'd also had enough interruptions, blurted "We're on our honeymoon!"

"Your honeymoon? Oh, you kids must be having a wonderful time." Mabel squinted her eyes. "I see you kids *are* having a wonderful time. Here, I'm just going to leave this welcome packet by the door. There's a 'Do Not Disturb' sign – you may want to consider using it."

Kristy and Rob looked at each other and shook their heads.

"Now, enjoy having all that honeymoon sex," said Mabel.

"What?" said Kristy.

"I know what a honeymoon is all about, my dear. I'm eighty years old, for goodness sakes. I've had more sex than you've had dinners."

Rob understood how Kristy felt when she fell into the nightstand. He'd never experienced such a sudden loss of interest.

"That reminds me, I'll have eggs and sausage prepared for breakfast. I don't know why, but it seems somehow appropriate. Enjoy your honeymoon, kids."

After Mabel closed the door, Rob turned to Kristy.

"Next time, we're staying at a hotel."

Going Down

During the summer months, teenagers flock to an amusement park located in the southern metro called ValleyFest. Filled with roller coasters, carnival games, and even a water park – it's a veritable cornucopia of youthful delights.

However, once the weather cools and the leaves begin to fall off the trees, the park transforms from a summer wonderland into a dark and ominous destination for thrillseekers that desire a more macabre environment. ValleyFest, or rather ValleyFright as it's known in the autumn months, was a busy, bustling hive of activity on a particular Saturday evening when Becky Conradi found herself visiting the park with several of her college friends.

Becky wasn't a native Minnesotan. If she had been, she would have been prepared with a much thicker jacket for early October. But to be fair, her friends were also significantly underdressed. For her friends, though, it was an intentional lack of clothing in order to pick up hot guys. For Becky, it was just poor planning. After all, she already had a boyfriend. And he just happened to be working at ValleyFright that particular evening.

Stacy, wearing a short skirt and high heel shoes, elbowed her in the ribs.

"Ow," said Becky. "What was that for?"

"Just trying to wake you up," said Stacy. "You're so busy looking for Seth that you barely noticed the super hot guys that just walked past us."

"That's the point," said Becky. "I already have Seth – I don't need any other hot guys. I just wish I knew where he's located tonight."

"What did you say he does here?"

"He's one of the costumed employees. He just walks around trying to scare the guests."

"What does he dress up as?" asked Stacy.

"A neon green skeleton," said Becky.

"Sexy."

"I just hope I find him soon," said Becky. "I'm so damn tired. I was up all night working on my senior thesis."

"Why do you bother? It's only October."

"I'm an overachiever," said Becky. "Besides, I always fear that something devastating will happen and I won't have time or energy to concentrate on the project later."

"Honey, if you get into a car wreck or something like that, you have bigger problems than not completing your thesis."

She had a point, but Becky couldn't help but be over-prepared. Except when it came to outerwear. She was *freezing*.

Becky suddenly noticed the distinct sound of Maroon 5. It seemed to be coming from Stacy's butt.

"I'm blowing up," said Stacy. She pulled a pink iPhone out of her back pocket. "Hey, girl – what's up? Oh sure. We'll meet you there. Got it."

"What's going on?" asked Becky.

"Tiff and Heather are going on the Uncorker. Have you been on that? Dang, that's a scary rollercoaster."

Becky shrugged.

"What's wrong?" asked Stacy.

"I guess I'm just not feeling it," said Becky.

"C'mon, Beck – live a little!"

"You go ahead," said Becky. "I'm going to keep looking for Seth."

"Why don't you just call your bony boyfriend? Find out where he is?"

Becky shook her head. "He's not allowed to answer his phone while on the job. He'll get fired."

"Alright," said Stacy. "Suit yourself. When you get bored of looking for your knight in neon green armor, come find me. You can always call me."

"Sounds good, Stace."

Becky watched Stacy meander away very slowly, clearly trying not to trip on her high heels. High heels were not part of Becky's wardrobe. She was purely a jeans and sneakers kind of girl.

As Becky walked down one of the central paths through the park, she kept her eyes peeled for neon green skeletons. Unfortunately, she was not seeing much more than a wolfman, a grim reaper, and a zombie. *Real original*, thought Becky.

She couldn't wait to find Seth. They'd been dating for nearly three months and this was her first opportunity to see him at his job. Like Becky, he was a senior sociology major, a big film buff, and wanted to start a family shortly after college. He was also an incredible lover, something that Becky never considered an important trait, but now that she had it, she couldn't imagine living without it.

With her own arms wrapped around her chest in a feeble attempt to try to keep warm, Becky turned a corner and nearly jumped out of her skin as a vampire went after her neck. She instinctively delivered a fist to the vampire's chest.

"What the hell?" exclaimed the vampire.

"Sorry, you surprised me," said Becky.

"No shit – that's gonna happen. It's a haunted amusement park."

"I said I'm sorry."

The vampire scowled and scampered off, looking for another victim with slower reflexes than Becky.

"Beeeecccky!"

She looked around. Someone had clearly called her name.

"Beeeeccky ahhhhhhhhh!"

Becky looked up and realized her friends were passing back and forth on the Uncorker roller coaster right above her head. Becky waved.

She turned a bend, hoping to see her neon hunk, but he was nowhere to be seen. Becky slowly shuffled towards a bench just off the walkway. She got really excited when she saw a figure on the bench that seemed somewhat skeleton-like, but it turned out to just be an old man with possible malnutrition issues.

Becky sighed. "Do you mind if I sit here?"

The old man grunted.

That was good enough for Becky. She sat on the bench and rubbed her arms up and down, trying to bring a little warmth back into them. She looked left and right, all the way down the cement path, hoping to see Seth, but it seemed hopeless. She was tired of walking. She was tired of being cold. She was just tired.

She thought about calling Stacy to see if she was ready to go home, but she didn't want to ruin her fun. Becky decided to rest her eyes. Just for a while.

***

Becky felt a bony finger touch her thigh. She had a panicked moment where she thought the old man on the bench was getting fresh with her, but when she opened her eyes and turned her head, there was no one there. When she turned her head the other way, she nearly had the pants scared right off her. Which would have been fine. Because it was Seth. He finally found her.

The neon green skeleton waved his hand.

"You scared the crap out of me," said Becky. "Do you know how long I was looking for you?"

The skeleton opened its arms for an embrace.

"Yes, please – it's frickin' freezing out here. Warm me up."

Although the costume wasn't the most pleasant to look at, he wasn't as cold as she was expecting a skeleton to be. He rubbed her bare arms up and down. He massaged her lower back. She kissed his mask.

"I suppose you're not allowed to take that off during the work day?"

The skeleton shook his head.

"How do you pee in that thing?"

The skeleton pulled aside a pelvic bone, revealing a zipper.

"Umm...maybe we could warm up somewhere? Do you know any good 'employee only' buildings we could get into?"

The skeleton nodded.

Becky grabbed his hand. He led her around the Uncorker, past a mini-donut stand, and into a small, restricted building. The skeleton removed a bone from his right buttock, exposing a pocket. He pulled a key out and inserted it into the doorknob. He opened the door.

Becky could see that it wasn't a terribly large space. It was filled with paper towels, cleaning supplies, toilet paper, napkins, food wrappers – any stock that the employees might need for their stands or the adjoining restrooms.

The skeleton held his thumbs up.

Becky laughed. "Sure, this will work." She put her arms around her loving boyfriend. She was so happy to be out of the cold and with someone who she could count on to warm her up.

The skeleton rubbed her back.

"Mmm, that feels good," said Becky. She returned the favor by massaging his thighs.

The skeleton groaned.

"Have you ever done anything like this before?" asked Becky.

The skeleton shook his head.

"How about like this?" asked Becky as she moved the front pelvic bone of the skeleton's suit aside, revealing the zipper beneath. She unzipped it.

"Like this idea?" asked Becky.

The skeleton vigorously nodded.

Becky reached in and pulled out the skeleton's most private bone. It did strike Becky as odd that Seth's fleshy member was shorter than she remembered, but it *was* cold, after all. She didn't fancy herself an expert on how those things work.

Becky proceeded to orally pleasure the skeleton.

The skeleton grunted and shook.

Becky paused. "Everything okay?"

Again, the skeleton nodded excitedly.

Becky was about to continue, but the skeleton offered an outstretched hand to her. She took his hand and he lifted her to her feet. In a swift move that Becky certainly wanted to take for romance, the skeleton spun Becky around and bent her over a box of cooking oil.

"Oh wow – I wasn't expecting this," said Becky.

The skeleton pulled down her shorts and underwear and went to town, figuratively speaking.

And just as fast as it started, it was over.

"Umm...are you okay?" asked Becky.

Becky turned around. The skeleton shrugged.

"Geez, Seth – I don't think you were ever that fast before. I guess you were just that excited, hmm?"

The skeleton remained motionless for a few

seconds. Then he began reaching for the doorknob.

"Wait – Seth. Where are you going? Why aren't you saying anything?"

A voice croaked out a few words with a high-pitched voice.

"I'm not Seth. I don't know who that is."

Becky's stomach lurched.

"I'm...sorry?" asked the skeleton, his voice cracking as he said it.

"Please take off your mask," said Becky.

The skeleton did so, revealing a young teenager with blond hair, acne scarring on his cheeks, and giant holes in his earlobes.

"Oh, Jesus," said Becky.

"I'm Trevor. I'm working here for the summer," he said. "I...umm, just thought you wanted to hook up. I didn't think you thought I was someone else."

"How many women just walk up to you and request sexual attention?"

Trevor smiled. "You'd be surprised. I think the Scrambler does something to women's hormones or something."

"Yuck."

"Sorry."

"Let's just pretend this didn't happen," said Becky.

Trevor shrugged. "Whatever."

"Do you know where I can find Seth?"

"I don't know who that is."

"He's also a neon green skeleton."

The lightbulb went on above Trevor's head. "Oh, that Seth. Yeah, he's the other skeleton. That explains why you mixed us up."

"Yeah, obviously," said Becky.

"He's definitely older and more handsome looking than I am," said Trevor. "I mean, I'm pretty good – but he's like super handsome."

"Thanks," said Becky, not quite sure how to respond.

"So anyway, he should be back by the Excelsior roller coaster. That's his turf."

"Great. Hey, can I get your phone number?" asked Becky.

"Was I good? You want to hook up again sometime?"

"No, but I do want to know who to contact if I end up getting some scorching venereal disease."

"Oh, right. I guess that makes sense," said Trevor.

***

As Becky walked along the cement path, following the signs that pointed towards the Excelsior roller coaster, she was mixed with emotions about what had transpired. On the one hand, she hadn't intentionally cheated on Seth – quite the opposite. She thought she was giving Seth one of the best nights at work he'd ever had. Unfortunately it turned into a classic sitcom mix-up. On the other hand, she couldn't blame Trevor. She hadn't called him Seth or asked him to take off his mask until the situation got...well, a bit sticky.

She was passing an ice cream stand covered in spiderwebs and fake bats when she heard a familiar voice.

Stacy was laughing along with Seth, who was holding his skeleton mask. They spotted Becky and ran over to her.

"Well, where have you been?" asked Seth. He had a smile on his face, but he was sweating. It looked like he had a long day of work. "I was looking all over for you."

"I figured you guys were out boning in the bushes," said Stacy. "Then I saw him stopping young kids from getting on the adult rides."

"It's a tough job," said Seth.

"But seriously, where were you this whole time?" asked Stacy. "Were you just going on rides by yourself?"

Becky coughed.

"You okay?" asked Seth.

"Yeah, yeah...I just, umm...have you ever had a really weird day?" asked Becky.

Seth laughed. "All the time around here. This place brings out people's freaky side."

"How so?" asked Stacy.

"Okay, so here's an example that's a little out there. So last fall, this fairy princess pulls me into a French fry stand towards the end of the night. She's all over me – I mean, things get intense."

"That's super hot," said Stacy.

Becky was cringing.

"Well, not exactly. I didn't find out until way too late that it was actually this creepy kid named Trevor who switches costumes each week. Talk about a surprise, right?"

"Damn," said Stacy.

"I know," said Seth.

Stacy looked at Becky. "So what was so weird about your night?"

Becky considered her options. "You know what? I fell asleep on a bench. Crazy, right?"

"Yeah, crazy," said Seth with a questioning eyebrow. "Well, I better get back to work. I'm not even supposed to have my mask off right now. I don't want to get in trouble."

On the Hunt

The bitter chill of the November air was omnipresent. It clung to everything, seeping in through jackets and clothes and skin and muscle. It was a silent enemy. One that was clever with how it went about its business. It stayed in the background. There was no wind to speak of and no snow pelting down. The shining sun gave a false sense of warmth that didn't translate to degrees above Fahrenheit. It was in this unshaken snowglobe where Ned Gorgonchuck found himself in a deer stand, bundled head to toe with orange winter garments, holding a rifle that he desperately hoped he'd get a chance to use.

Ned hailed from a small town in southern Minnesota where he worked at a meat processing plant. It wasn't glamorous work by any means, but it was good enough to get him by. But one thing that kept him going during the daily grind of carcass rendering was the knowledge that every autumn, he'd have the chance to take a vacation from his job and sit in the woods. He knew it probably sounded boring to most folks, but simply to breathe in cold, clean air instead of a cattle's internal gasses was a blessing.

He did, however, like at least a little action during deer hunting season. So far he'd been sitting in his tree stand for three days and hadn't seen a single thing. Even with a nice coating of snow on the ground, he'd barely seen so much as a hoof print. Even though he had a cooler full of PBR's, Ned was starting to get *bored*.

Despite his plentiful layers of clothing, the cold was getting to him. He had thick gloves on, but his fingers were still growing numb. He reached into his backpack. His mom had packed some pressure-activated gel hand-warmers for him. His mom always packed his backpack for him the day before he left hunting. Ever since he was a kid.

After removing his gloves, Ned took one of the hand-warmer packs and twisted it until he could feel the gel had activated. Within seconds, intense heat emanated from the gel pack. It felt good. He could feel some life coming back into his cold, pale hand.

That's when he got the idea.

It wasn't necessarily a good idea, or even a terribly original idea. But Ned was bored and more than a little drunk. And if he wasn't having any luck firing off *that* gun, well...

Ned unzipped his pants. Into his pants he inserted the warm gel pack.

It felt good. Really good. In fact, he found himself getting rather carried away. Within a couple minutes, he was done. Unfortunately, he'd made a bit of a mess on his orange jacket. He looked like a Dreamsicle.

"Oh, cripes," said Ned, as he peered into his backpack. To his chagrin, he didn't have a single pack of tissues. "Dammit, Mom."

Sighing deeply, Ned resigned himself to the fact that masturbating in the woods was the most fun he'd had in a full year. With that profound thought swimming through his brain, Ned drifted off into a deep sleep.

***

When Ned awoke, he had trouble seeing much of anything. It had begun to snow after he fell asleep, and he himself was covered in a thin layer of snow. Ned decided that, after getting distracted for the past couple hours (or was it a few hours? Maybe more?), he was going to rededicate himself to finding and shooting a deer.

It was a noble goal. But as time ticked by, and after consuming his final six PBR's, he found himself once again bored. And, as such things so often happen in the world, history repeated itself.

Ned's hand, firmly gripping a gel hand-warmer, was once again in his pants. This time, however, it took a bit longer and involved a little additional exertion. He was also rather vocal.

As Ned reached closer and closer to climax, he was suddenly pulled out of his activity by the sound of a distinct clicking sound. "Oh, shit."

Ned looked down from the deer stand towards the snow-covered ground. He saw a bright orange figure standing with a rifle pointed directly at him. "Don't shoot!"

The person holding the rifle immediately lowered it.

"Sorry about that," Ned heard a feminine voice say. "I heard a strange sound coming from this direction. I thought maybe there was some kind of mongoose caught in a bear trap or something."

"That was just me," said Ned. "I was jus...trying to dry off my gun. All this damn snow. Am I right?" Ned quickly reinserted his manhood back into his pants while he was still mostly out of direct eyesight from the woman down below.

"Okay," said the woman skeptically.

"Who are you?" asked Ned, zipping up.

"I'm Dawn," she said. "My stand is like a hundred yards that way."

"Why are you all the way out here by my stand?"

"Like I said, I heard the funny sounds. But I was already walking around. I haven't seen a dang deer anywhere."

"I know what you mean," said Ned.

Dawn stood silent for a moment.

"Want some company?" she asked.

Ned, wanting to play it cool, said, "Yeah, sure – you know, whatever." At that moment he realized that underneath the snow on his jacket was a thick crust of baby batter. "Oh, sumbitch," he muttered as he frantically wiped and scraped at the front of his jacket.

"Everything okay?" asked Dawn.

"Oh, yeah – c'mon up," said Ned.

As Dawn ascended the ladder of the deer stand,

Ned could see she was pretty, if not a little on the older side.

"You been hunting long?" asked Ned.

"All my life," she said. "My stand down yonder was my daddy's till he passed away a few years back. He hadn't hunted for years, though. Used to take my husband out here, but that ended a couple years ago."

"The hunting?"

"No, the marriage. Speaking of which, got any extra beers in that cooler of yours?"

Ned winced. "Sorry...that's been the one thing that's been keeping me occupied up here."

"It's okay," said Dawn. "I always run out, too." Dawn brushed aside some snow on the wood planks of the floor next to Ned. She sat down right by him.

"Girlfriend or wife?" asked Dawn.

Ned shook his head. "Naw. I work a lot. It's hard to meet someone."

"Nothing wrong with that. What do you do? For work?"

"Nothing important," said Ned.

"I'm curious, though," said Dawn. "What is it?"

Ned shrugged. "I work in a meat processing plant. I break down the carcasses into consumable and non-consumable parts. It's not terribly exciting."

"Are you kidding?" asked Dawn. "Can you process your own deer?"

"Sure," said Ned. "That's about the only perk of the job."

"That's a pretty big turn on."

Ned cocked his eyebrow. "Really?" He'd never

heard that one before.

She nodded her head. "Yeah."

Ned swallowed hard. "Umm...do you...want –"

Before Ned could finish, Dawn was on top of him, pressing her lips against his. She kissed him hard, pressing her body against his. Ned could feel the heat radiating from her. In the middle of such a frigid environment, the warmth that Dawn exuded was an unexpected and pleasant surprise.

As Dawn's hands explored the contours of his body, Ned found himself getting aroused again. Dawn reached for his zipper. She pulled the zipper down. Her hand entered his pants and left with a small gel-pack in her hand. "What is *this?*"

"Hand warmer," responded Ned.

"In your pants?"

Ned shrugged. "It was chilly."

Dawn laughed. "Nothing wrong with that. I bet I can make it a lot warmer than that old thing, though."

"Really?"

Dawn smiled.

"What...umm, are you going to –"

Dawn pulled down Ned's pants and underwear, and then did the same herself. Within mere moments, she was on top of Ned, mounting him passionately and rhythmically.

"This is the most fun I've ever –" Ned paused to grunt, "had while hunting before. Phew."

"You have good aim," said Dawn, panting, continuing to grind her hips against his. Ned would have agreed, but his face was buried firmly in her partially-unzipped parka-covered chest.

Dawn's voice grew louder. Ned was thrilled that Dawn was enjoying herself, and that it required virtually no effort on his part. *What a great day*, thought Ned.

Then it happened. A sound like a gunshot. Then falling. Falling. OOOOOPH.

Dawn was groaning beside him – definitely *not* in a good way. Ned also felt sharp pain in his back. Ned had enough awareness to realize the deer stand gave way under the weight of two not-terribly-thin people creating a lot of force and friction on old wooden boards. Ned would have kept up the condition of the deer stand, but he had never foreseen this scenario.

The pain in his back – did he break something? No, just wood fragment digging into his flesh. Did Dawn have the same issue? He rolled over so he was facing her. Nope, her problems were much worse. Her left leg seemed to be bent and twisted in an unnatural state.

"What happened?" croaked Dawn. "Were we shot?"

"No," said Ned. "The deer stand fell."

"I hurt so bad," said Dawn.

"Yeah, you got a little banged up," said Ned.

"I'm freezing."

"You're lying in a snowbank with your pants around your ankles. That'll make you a bit chilly."

"Can you help me up?" asked Dawn.

"Yeah, about that..."

"What?"

Ned grimaced as he pulled a thick splinter out of

his arm. "I don't think you'll be running a marathon anytime soon."

Dawn looked down and screamed.

"Settle down, settle down," said Ned. "Looks like a broken leg. It will take a while to heal, but you should be fine."

"Just get me out of here," said Dawn. "Please."

"Yeah, of course. My pick-up is about thirty yards from here."

"Shit," said Dawn. Even two yards would have felt like too far to move.

"I have a blanket in there. I could lay that out on the snow and use it to drag you."

"I don't think that's going to work," said Dawn.

"Why not?"

"Because that involves you leaving me alone, half naked, in the middle of the woods, while you go get a blanket from your truck."

"Your rifle is around here somewhere," said Ned, as he spotted it resting against a tree. "You can hold onto that while I go get the blanket."

"Nope," said Dawn. "Not happening. Stay with me."

Ned nodded. "Okay. Well, we can't get your pants up, what with how your leg is all twisted up like a piece of licorice.

"What should we do?"

Ned unzipped his parka.

"I don't think now is an appropriate time for that," said Dawn.

Ned smirked. "I'm going to take off my shirt and

put it under your butt. That way your back end won't be scraping against rocks and twigs and whatnot."

Dawn smiled. "That's the sweetest thing anyone's ever done for me."

"The least I can do. You gave me the most exciting day of deer hunting I've ever had."

Dawn laughed, then grinded her teeth in pain. "Don't make me laugh anymore."

Ned unbuttoned his flannel shirt, removed it, then placed it underneath Dawn. He rubbed his arms. "Bit brisk out here isn't it?"

"At least you have pants on," said Dawn.

Ned rubbed his chin. "I have an idea. Your pants right now aren't serving a purpose around your ankles. How about I take them off and use them to tie your rifle against your leg like a splint? That way we shouldn't damage your leg too much while I drag you through the woods."

Dawn nodded. "Okay, let's do it."

Ned put his jacket back on first, then tied up the makeshift rifle splint, just like he'd suggested.

"I have a feeling this is still going to be painful," said Dawn.

"You're probably right," said Ned. "But I will drag you slowly as possible, so hopefully you'll feel very little.'

"Okay," said Dawn, bracing herself for the start of their journey towards the pick-up truck.

"Ready?" asked Ned.

Dawn nodded. "Let's go."

Ned held onto Dawn's outstretched arms, pulling her gently along the snow. There were a few literal bumps in their journey, which Dawn responded to with several expletives, including a few choice ones that Ned had never heard before. They had also lost the shirt underneath Dawn's butt twice.

As the pick-up truck came within view, Dawn was both relieved and nervous. She knew getting into the pick-up would be neither easy nor pain-free.

"I hate to say it," said Ned, "but I think we need to load you up in the back of the truck. There's no way we can get you in a decent position in the passenger seat."

Dawn gulped. "I had the same feeling."

Ned pulled Dawn close to the tailgate, then gently laid her down on the snow. He unlatched the tailgate and let it down. He took one arm and began pushing out as much snow from the truck as he could.

"I can't get all the snow out of here," said Ned, "but hopefully it will be clear enough for you."

"I don't care," said Dawn. "Just get me to the hospital."

"Okay, I think the only way we get do this is if you put pressure on your good leg while I pull you into the truck. Alright?"

"Yeah, okay," said Dawn, nodding. Dawn grimaced as Ned lifted and pulled her into the vehicle. At one point her bad leg hit the edge of the tailgate and Dawn whimpered in pain.

"Sorry," said Ned, pulling her all way back into the truck. He lifted and latched the tailgate. "Ready for a ride?"

"For the love of God," said Dawn, "drive carefully."

"I will," said Ned, hoping that Dawn didn't

recognize the whiskey plates on the back of his pick-up. Ned grinned. That thought gave Ned an idea. He reached into his glove box and pulled out a flask. He handed it to Dawn. "Don't drink too much of this. This here is some top-grade grain alcohol my buddy Mick made. This shit will knock you right on your a—"

By the time Ned finished his sentence, Dawn was chugging down the contents.

"I'll leave you be," said Ned. He crawled into the driver's seat and started up the truck.

***

As Ned drove along the highway, he got deep into thought about what an extraordinarily odd day he'd had. The day had started as just another low-key, boring morning of hunting. Then things took a weird turn. It was funny to think that, had he not started pleasuring himself with gel packs, Dawn may have never noticed his voice. *Just goes to show you*, thought Ned. *Sometimes, a little wanky wanky isn't such a bad —*

Suddenly, a deer leaped in front of Ned's truck. His left headlight smashed into the back half of the deer. "Holy shit," yelled Ned.

"What was that?" screamed Dawn from the rear of the truck.

"Just a deer," said Ned. "Just ruined a headlight. Nothing to worry about." Ned slowly drove the truck onto the shoulder of the highway.

"What are you doing?" yelled Dawn.

"Getting a look at the deer," said Ned. "It

looked like a decent size."

"But why –"

Ned got out of the truck and approached the deer. It wasn't moving. A thick stream of blood leaked from the deer's abdomen. It was a good size. Lots of meat.

He began dragging the deer.

***

Dawn was in pain. It didn't help that Ned – who she'd really come to like, despite some odd tendencies – kept hitting potholes that made Dawn's leg bounce and send sharp pain throughout her body.

To make matters worse, she now had a deer's hooves tickling the top of her head. Ned had strapped the deer to the top of the pick-up with the legs hanging down within inches of Dawn's face.

With little other options, Dawn uncapped the flask and took down the last few big gulps.

***

Ned saw a sign for the hospital at the upcoming exit. He was about to ask Dawn how she was faring when he saw blue and red lights coming up behind him. *Shit*, he thought.

He pulled over. Within seconds, a police officer approached his pick-up truck. Ned assumed the cop would come up to his window and speak with him, but instead the cop spent an extensive amount of time looking at the truck and its contents.

I might be in trouble, thought Ned.

After several minutes, the police officer approached Ned's window.

"Sir, can I see your identification please?"

Ned already had it prepared. He handed it to the cop.

"Great. Please step out of the vehicle, sir."

"Is everything okay?" asked Ned.

"Just step out now, please."

Ned did as instructed.

The police officer pointed at the deer. "Where did you get that?"

"I...umm...shot it?" said Ned with a distinct lack of confidence.

"You realize that hitting a deer and taking it with you is illegal in the state of Minnesota. Did you know that?"

"Sorry, I'm not aware of that. But I definitely shot it."

"Sir, there is a giant fender-shaped wound on this deer. It might also explain your single headlight, which is also illegal."

"Oh," said Ned.

"One other thing," said the police officer. "How do you explain the half-naked unconscious woman in the back of your truck?"

"Unconscious?" asked Ned. *Shit, she must have downed the whole flask*, he thought.

"Yessir," said the cop. "She looks awfully hurt. Did you run into her, too? Decide to keep her for yourself?"

"No, no, no!" said Ned, panicked. "She fell out

of my deer stand!"

"She fell out of your deer stand," said the police officer.

"Yes, honest! We were having sex, and the deer stand broke, and we fell to the ground and she broke her leg. That's exactly what happened."

"That's a pretty elaborate story," said the police officer. "Try coming up with a better explanation before we get downtown."

"Downtown?"

"You're under arrest."

"For what?" asked Ned.

"Look at all this," said the police officer, motioning his hand in the direction of the pick-up truck. "You're under arrest for all of *this*. I don't even know where to start."

"You believe me, right? The deer stand?"

"Sure, sure – the deer stand. Whatever you say, pal."

Ballin' at the Mall

Tessa Nygard had worked at the Mall of America since its inception in the early nineties. At first it was exciting – she was a young girl with a well-paying job in one of the busiest, bustling buildings in the Midwest. After a couple decades, her job became more tedious than exciting. Her profession itself – a mall cop – had become commonly mocked in TV and movies. A few years back, there had been a reality show that took place in the Mall of America about mall cops. Tessa was featured in one episode. She helped Old Man Murphy, one of the crazy old geezers that frequented the mall all day, every day, with finding his hearing aide. He'd left it on his lunch tray from the Pandra Express, right next to the sweet and sour sauce.

As with many folks who've become less-enchanted with their jobs over the years, Tessa found herself making choices outside of the realm of what she'd consider normal. Case in point: she began having a sexual relationship with a chiseled young man from

Abercrombie and Fitch. It wasn't exactly a scandal-of-the-year. Tessa was divorced, had a teenage child who was almost out of the house, and her daily life had become somewhat blasé. But still, since the sex tended to be during the work day, it put her career somewhat in jeopardy...

"I don't think we should be doing this anymore," said Tessa. They were lying in each others' arms behind a temporary façade in front of what had once been a Spencer's Gifts but would soon be the mall's third Hot Topic.

"Why?" asked Dylon, scratching his perfectly sculpted abs. "Like, am I not strong enough or something?"

"No, no – God, no," said Tessa. "Seriously, have you seen yourself? No, I just don't want to lose my job."

Dylon shrugged. "Doesn't seem like a big deal. You can always get another job."

"I can't take the risk," said Tessa. "I just don't want anyone to find out about this."

"Oh, man," said Dylon.

Tessa cocked her eyebrow. "What...what does that mean?"

"Well, it's like this...I, umm...already told a bunch of people?"

Tessa rubbed her forehead. She wanted to be angry, but she knew she couldn't be angry at Dylon. He was an idiot. It wasn't his fault – it was just nature. But she should have known better.

"How many people, Dylon? Who?"

"Oh, umm...like, everyone at Abercrombie, right?

Cuz I work there and we talk about stuff? Some of the customers, too."

"Why?"

"I dunno, just something to talk about, I guess?"

At that moment, they were interrupted by a loud, rapid knocking on the door of the façade.

"What was that?" asked Dylon. "Are we under attack?"

"I don't think so," said Tessa. "Let me go check."

Tessa wrapped herself in her unbuttoned uniform. She approached the façade, but didn't dare open the door. "Who is it?"

She heard a strained voice say, "Are you the singer girl? Is this where the concert is?"

Tessa rolled her eyes. There was going to be a performance by Ariana Grande at the pavilion on the lower level of the mall. Performances – especially the ones for a younger crowd – always brought out a few weirdos. Fortunately, this was one weirdo she knew – Old Man Murphy.

"Murphy, go down the escalators. You'll see a whole bunch of people waiting by a stage. That's the concert."

"Not here?" she heard Old Man Murphy ask.

"No, downstairs."

"Oy, oy," he said. "Downward we go."

"Okay," said Tessa. She walked back over to where Dylon was lying down, still naked next to a pile of clothes. Tessa sat down. "Listen, Dylon – you're a really sweet kid. I think you should date some other girls, though. Maybe more your age."

"That's cool – I mean, I have been already. We

weren't like...a thing, were we?"

Tessa shook her head."No, no we weren't. Go back to your life and keep being you, Dylon."

"Okay, cool," said Dylon, as he stood up and pulled on his artificially faded designer jeans.

Tessa put her uniform back on. She knew that her relationship with Dylon wasn't anything real, but it didn't make her feel any less sad.

"I better get back to the store or Monica's gonna kill me," said Dylon. "She said if I keep banging every mall employee except her, she's going to fire me."

"That's terrible, Dylon – that's sexual harassment."

"Yeah, I can't really say anything, though," said Dylon.

"Why not?"

"When she interviewed me, I told her she has really nice cans and that I'd like to squeeze them because they're so nice. Think she could use that against me?"

Tessa thought of how to respond, then just said, "Why don't you get going, Dylon. Have a good night at work."

"You too, Tessa," he said. "I really like you. You're a cool cop."

"Thanks."

Tessa watched as Dylon put on an overly-tight t-shirt and walked out of the side door of the façade. She shook her head. It was really nice being with him, but it had to end sometime. Tessa finished buttoning up her shirt and walked out the same side door.

Tessa nearly walked into the crowd of passing mall patrons when she had the sudden, sharp realization that something was missing. She looked down at herself. Her clothes were on, so that was a plus. Her belt – complete with flashlight, nightstick, and handcuffs – was firmly attached. No, there was something else missing. Something really...*shit.*

Her Segway. The senior-level mall cops were given Segways within the past few years to help with speed when catching criminals and also to decrease work-injury, which was common with how much time the mall cops spent on their feet. It was a really good idea. Useful. That is, when the particular mall cops maintained possession of their respective Segway.

She had a couple options. She could call her boss, Chief Gurski, and let him know that her Segway was stolen. Of course, that would lead to questions. Questions could lead to review of video surveillance. She doubted there were any cameras within the remodeled store space, but certainly anyone watching the walkway surveillance would notice Tessa and Dylon disappearing into the same area for...oh, about twenty five minutes, give or take. Her Segway had been sitting right outside the side door to the façade. Surveillance would show who took it. It would also show enough evidence that Tessa was not doing her job and she would be fired.

Tessa decided to find her Segway herself before Chief Gurski knew anything was amiss.

***

After Tessa had covered most of the third floor from which the Segway was so boldly stolen, she realized that any thief would have likely headed directly to an elevator. In fact, she likely wasted twenty critical minutes fruitless searching the wrong floor. *Dammit.*

She ran down a nearby escalator, excusing herself as she pushed by shoppers. As she reached the bottom, a voice exuded from her walkie talkie.

"Officer Nygard? Officer Nygard? Please copy."

"Copy that," said Tessa, holding the walkie to her mouth. To her dismay, she could tell it was Chief Gurski.

"Please report to the Abercrombie and Fitch on the 3rd floor. I understand you are nearby. Please confirm."

Tessa felt her heart drop. Did Gurski know about her relationship with Dylon? Or that it was during work hours?

"Confirmed," said Tessa."I will be at the location within three minutes."

"10-4," concluded Gurski.

Tessa turned around and went right back on the escalator headed up. The shoppers she had just brushed past on the way down gave her questioning stares.

The Abercrombie was near the escalator, just opposite the in-development store where she and Dylon frequently made love. When she arrived, she was expecting to see Chief Gurski standing there with her dismissal papers in his hand. Instead, he found a distraught Dylon.

"All...gone," he said.

"What's gone?" asked Tessa.

"All of them," he repeated."All gone."

"What are you talking about, Dylon?" asked Tessa. "Who? What? What's gone?"

Dylon looked up as though he had just understood her question. "The turtlenecks."

"What?" asked Tessa.

"Every turtleneck in the store. Gone," said Dylon.

"Are you the one who called security?" asked Tessa.

Dylon nodded.

"Isn't your boss around. Monica?"

Dylon shook his head. "When I got here, there weren't any employees. Just me. And the turtlenecks...they were already gone."

"So anyone could have left with the merchandise," said Tessa.

Dylon nodded. "Who would do such a thing?"

"I don't know," said Tessa. "But we'll catch whoever it is."

"I've never seen anything like it," said Dylon, looking eerily similar to an Iraq war veteran recouping from PTSD.

"Dylon, is there any security cam footage?"

He nodded. "I think so. It's usually running. I can get the tapes."

"Great," said Tessa. "Do that. In the meantime, I have another...thing I have to do."

"More important than this?" asked Dylon.

"Well, maybe," said Tessa. She debating confiding in Dylon about the stolen Segway, but ultimately she decided *Ahh, screw it – we broke up.* "I'll be back soon. Get those tapes."

Dylon nodded.

***

Tessa was about to head back down to the second floor when her walkie crackled and spoke to her once again. "Officer Nygard? Are you present?"

"Yes, copy that," said Tessa.

"We just received a threat regarding the Ariana Grande concert at the pavilion. It sounds credible. I want you to go to the concert and see if anything is amiss."

"Chief – I'm already dealing with a theft at the Abercrombie. Isn't someone else available?"

"Sorry, Nygard – it's a tight ship today."

"What was the threat?" asked Tessa.

"The caller stated that the 'sinful crowd' watching the show would see much more flesh than they bargained for," said Glurski.

"What does that even mean?" asked Tessa. "And why is it credible?"

"The call came from within the mall," said Glurski. "Not even a cell phone – like, an actual landline within the mall. Not sure what it means, but look for anything suspicious."

"Anything recognizable or traceable about the caller?"

"It was a female," said Glurski. "So that's something."

"10-4," said Tessa.

Tessa went down yet another escalator to the first floor and bee-lined it for the pavilion. She could hear from the pumped up techno beats that the concert was already going.

The pavilion area was full of pre-teen girls clamoring to get a closer look at the star performer. Ariana had a good voice and an even better stage presence. Such a combination usually brought out a lot of interesting fans. She was wondering what or who she might see in the crowd for this particular show.

Admittedly, Tessa was searching the crowd for the obvious bad guys. She didn't see anyone or anything suspicious. That was, until her Segway showed up.

Old Man Murphy, with as much grace and poise as you would expect from a lonely Alzheimer's sufferer with poor social skills and even worse physical coordination, approached the pavilion area on the Segway. His pants were firmly resting around his ankles.

Tessa had to react fast. There was nothing appropriate about the whole situation. But something wasn't sitting with her quite right. She had seen Old Man Murphy hundreds of times over the last several years. He was always a bit strange – forgetful, lost, talking about things that happened thirty years ago – but he'd never exposed himself before. Something was wrong about this.

"I need back-up," said Tessa into her walkie. "Old Man Murphy is exposing himself to the crowd. We need to remove him from the area immediately."

"Shit," she heard Chief Glurski respond. "I'll be there in a minute. Do your best to separate him from the crowd. Or get his pants up. Something."

"Copy that," said Tessa.

People with horrified looks on their faces were already backing away from Old Man Murphy. It made it real easy for Tessa to dart in front of them and approach Old Man Murphy head on.

"Pull your pants up," said Tessa.

"Tessa!" he responded. "Are you here for the show?"

"For God sakes, pull your pants up. Why are you doing this?" asked Tessa, pointing at his exposed genitals.

Old Man Murphy looked down at himself. He looked confused. Then he seemed to have a memory flash in his head. "That woman told me to," he said. "She said everyone would be showing off. It is the nineties, after all."

"This is illegal," said Tessa. "Pull them up right now."

"Okay," he said, reaching down.

"Hey, why did you take my Segway?"

"What?" asked Old Man Murphy, buckling his belt.

"My Segway. You're standing on it right now. Why?"

"She told me it was mine. She told me all VIP mall shoppers got one."

Tessa stared at Old Man Murphy intently. "Who is she?"

"You know," he said. "The lady. From the clothing store with the young boys."

"Abercrombie?"

"That's the one," he said. "They sure like posters with exposed abs in that store. She told me that all the kids just walk around naked nowadays. She told me to come down here and show off a bit."

"That's not true," said Tessa. "She was trying to take advantage of you."

"Oh," said Old Man Murphy, lowering his head.

Glurski showed up, out of breath. He had huffed it all the way from the security office at the opposite end of the mall. He was holding out handcuffs, ready to put them on Old Man Murphy. Tessa shook her head.

"Why not?" asked Chief Glurski.

Tessa whispered in Glurski ear. "Elder abuse," she said.

"Who? What?" asked Glurski.

"If I'm right, her name is Monica. She is the manager of the Abercrombie and Fitch on the 3rd floor. I didn't realize it til just now, but I believe she called in the threat. In addition, I believe she stole a great deal of merchandise from her store. I have an employee pulling the security footage right now."

"What does she have to with Old Man Murphy?"

"She convinced him to come here and expose himself."

"Why?"

"Distraction," said Tessa. "It gave her plenty more time to escape with the merchandise."

"Why is he standing on your Segway?"

Old Man Murphy began talking, but Tessa cut him off. "I figured the front of it might cover his private area until he was able to pull his pants up."

Glurski studied Tessa. "Good job," he responded.

"Shall we go see the security cam footage?" asked Tessa.

Glurski nodded. "Let's take your Segway. Running all this way sort of took it out of me."

"Okay," said Tessa. She whispered in Old Man Murphy's ear, "You should go home now. Don't get into any more trouble."

He nodded. He seemed to understand.

"Can I ride on the back with you?" asked Glurski, stepping onto the Segway right behind Tessa.

"Umm...sure?" said Tessa.

"I'm tuckered," he said. "Thank you."

***

As the Segway that contained Tessa and Glurski made its way to the Abercrombie and Fitch, Glurski said, "Listen, Tessa – there have been a lot of rumors circulating lately."

"Oh?" she asked, feeling her stomach tighten.

"I don't care to be involved in any of that talk," said Glurski. "Just make sure that whatever you do, it doesn't interfere with your job. Got it?"

"Got it," said Tessa. After a moment of hesitation, "Thank you."

Tessa and Glurski entered the Abercrombie. Dylon was still standing in front of the store, looking bewildered.

"Any news?" asked Tessa. "Did you find the footage?"

Dylon nodded. "I did. It was Monica. She didn't even try to hide it."

Dylon brought Tessa and Glurski back into the employee office. He showed them the footage on a thirteen-inch black and white monitor.

"All this for turtlenecks?" asked Glurski.

Dylon nodded. "It's worth it, too."

"Why do you say that, son?"

Tessa smirked at Glurski's condescending tone.

"The turtlenecks – they're each worth about $200," said Dylon.

"How many did she steal?"

"About 200," said Dylon.

"That's like..." Glurski attempted to count on his fingers, "four thousand dollars."

"Forty thousand," said Tessa. "Not bad. But enough to sacrifice your job over?"

"I'm pretty sure she was getting fired anyway," said Dylon. "Money has been missing over the last few months. It seems obvious now that it was her."

"I can't believe she called in a threat and convinced Old Man Murphy to expose himself just for the sake of some turtleneck sweaters," said Tessa.

"Old Man Murphy exposed himself?" asked Dylon. "Whoa."

"Well, at least this case is closed," said Glurski.

"Yes," said Tessa. "This day has been too weird."

Tessa was turning to leave on the Segway with Glurski holding her tight.

"Hey Tessa?" asked Dylon.

Tessa turned the Segway around. "Yes?"

"You sure you don't want to have sex anymore?"

Tessa looked behind her at Glurski. He feigned ignorance and covered his ears with his hands.

"I don't think so, Dylon. Sorry."

As she drove away on the Segway, she looked behind her one more time. Dylon looked sad.

"Dylon?"

"Yeah?"

Tessa swallowed. "Why don't you give me a call later."

Dylon laughed. "Cool."

State of Affairs

"I don't get it," said Mark, looking down at a map of the State Fair, which was getting wet from rain pelting down on it. "This place seems to go on for miles. And it's mostly food. Why not just go to a grocery store?"

Ashley adjusted her red raincoat. "Are you kidding? The State Fair is amazing! The cute animals, the deep-fried yummies, the live music, the rides and games...I love this place so much."

"So you've been here a couple times?" asked Mark. This was their third date after meeting on an internet dating site. He realized that there was still a lot to learn about Ashley.

"I've come here every year since I was a little girl." She smiled. It struck Mark that she was likely recalling some fond memories.

"Well, I'm not sold on it yet, but I'm willing to give it a shot," said Mark. "How bad could it be?"

"That's the spirit," said Ashley. "Now let's head down towards the Grandstand. There's this fantastic gyro stand called Demitri's. I have to have one!"

"Whatever," said Mark. "I mean – yeah, cool. That sounds good."

Thunder crashed overhead and a torrent of rain began downpouring from the sky.

"Boy, this weather is not looking good," said Mark. "Are you sure you want to stay for a long time?"

Ashley shrugged. "The rain usually makes my hair crazy, but other than that – I don't mind. Besides, we're already here. We're not leaving until the button on my jeans pops off."

"Huh," said Mark. "Okay." He'd never heard a girl talk about food consumption in such a fashion. "Well, can we at least get out of the rain?"

"Yeah, sure," said Ashley. "Actually, if we hop on the Sky Ride, that's the quickest way to the Grandstand. We'll be out of the rain."

"Alright," said Mark.

Ashley led him to the end of the zip line that extended from the northeast corner of the fair to the southwest corner of the fair. A seemingly endless number of enclosed metal chairs were circulating along the line.

"So we just ride this all the way there?"

"Yeah," said Ashley.

Mark nodded. "Alright, sounds good."

As they got towards the front of the line, Mark handed a few bucks to the ride operator. He was excited to get out of the rain, even if only for a few minutes. The operator directed them to one of the empty cars that had just arrived.

"The seat's wet," said Mark.

"Who cares," said Ashley. "Let's go for it."

Shortly after sitting down in the moist bucket, the ride began to move, lifting Mark and Ashley into the air, several yards above the ground.

Mark could see that the rain had dampened the top of Ashley's white t-shirt beneath her raincoat. It made him curious what the rest of the shirt looked like. He wanted to see more. So he did the only reasonable thing he could think of – he unbuttoned her coat and removed it. As he did so, Ashley looked at him with a mixture of bemusement and excitement.

"What do you think you're doing?" asked Ashley, flexing her back to provide the best view.

"Nothing," said Mark. "Thought I'd just take a look." He reviewed what dangled in front him. Two tantalizing small globes wrapped beneath a cotton shirt, like two napkin-covered candied apples.

Ashley put an arm around his neck and pulled him in, locking her lips with his. With her eyes closed, she felt his arms wrap around her. Then his hands went lower, pulling at her shirt and lifting it over her head.

Mark was pleased to find that Ashley was returning the favor. His shirt disappeared and within seconds, she was yanking at his belt and pulling down his jeans. He was just aware enough to realize that they were plenty far away from the exit. Besides, the frequent stops to load and unload the cars gave them ample time to have their own great Minnesota get-together.

Ashley kneeled down within the car and proceeded to treat Mark's manhood as though it was a Pronto Pup with a fresh slathering of ketchup and mustard.

After a minute of enjoying what Ashley had to offer, Mark decided he could resist no longer and lifted Ashley from her kneeling position, turned her around, and bent her over. Soon, he was like a Greek food vendor, filling her pita with tzatziki sauce.

To his surprise, Mark was beginning to enjoy the fair.

As Mark was mid-thrust, the Sky Ride came to a sudden stop. They'd endured several stops on their journey through the air of the State Fair, but being as this was their first stop in the standing position – standing on a slick metal floor, no less – Mark lost his balance.

Mark tumbled out of the Sky Ride. Ashley made one feeble attempt to save him, but instead caught the jeans that were around his ankles. Mark's feet disappeared from them, but Ashley still held firmly onto the jeans as she screamed.

Pummeling bare-ass naked through the air, Mark's first instinct was to assume he was a goner. He'd hit something hard and that would be it – lights out. He was surprised to find that his fall only lasted a second. He didn't make it all the way to the ground. Instead, he slammed onto a wet, slick, metallic surface. His body kept moving, making a sickly squeaky rubbing sound. As little kids whizzed by him on mats, he realized where he was.

Mark heard the gasps as his naked body approached the bottom of the Giant Slide.

Everything that followed seemed like a dream. A very bad dream. Where he was in a populated area with no clothes on. People moved away from him. Parents grabbed their children and covered their eyes. He saw one mother press a funnel cake into her child's face to prevent the little girl from seeing his nakedness.

Security officers seemed to emerge from nowhere. They had their eyes on Mark. They probably didn't like supposed perverts hopping on kid rides with their dingily-dangilies exposed. There was no easy way to explain this situation, and Mark really didn't want to try. So instead, he ran.

He pushed through the crowd. Earlier he had found this chore to be extraordinarily difficult, but with his current lack of clothes, people were more than obliged to move out of the way for him.

Mark clutched his genitals as he stealthily moved through swarms of people. Some, the younger crowd mostly, giggled when they caught a glimpse of him. Not all were so affable. An older lady ruthlessly poked his abdomen with her cane until he could work his way around a traffic jam of strollers. He had no choice but to jump over a stroller with a young kid munching on cotton candy. It was not his proudest moment.

A hand pressed into his chest.

"Hold on there, son," he heard a voice say.

Mark was going to brush right past him, but the man grabbed his wrist. It was an older gentleman. He was holding an American Flag umbrella with his other hand. He had a kind face, but seemed distraught.

"I'm not sure if you're aware of this, junior – but you've got no clothes on."

"Yeah, I know – I have to get out of here!

Let me go..."

"You're not on the methamphetamines, are you son? You kids are getting all hopped up on that stuff and stealin' and gettin' naked and whatnot."

"I'm not on drugs! I'm just dealing with some very peculiar circumstances. I need to get away from all these people before someone decks me."

"You may want to take some shelter while you figure it out, young man. I'd suggest one of them buildings over there." The old man motioned toward a series of concession booths.

Mark nodded. "Yeah, okay."

The old man released his hand and Mark scurried along towards the first booth he came across. It was a tiny Pronto Pup stand. Although it was somewhat enclosed, he didn't like the idea of his manhood being so close to a vat of oil that typically cooked oblong objects.

The rain was starting to come down even harder. Mark knew he had very little time to think – he just had to move. His body had become slick with rain. He was getting cold. He wanted to be far away from the angry, judging eyes of the fairgoers and figure things out.

The next stand he came across also cooked oblong objects, but provided far more room and more seclusion. The Deep-Fried Candy Bar booth was huge – nearly three times the size of the Pronto Pup booth. Maybe once he got there and hid amongst their stock of napkins and whatnot, he'd be able to convince an employee to buy him a shirt from a vendor. A really long t-shirt.

The line for deep-fried Snickers, Three Musketeers, and Oreos was twenty-people deep, and Mark didn't have time to politely wait for a chance to ask for shelter and maybe an article of clothing. So instead he did the only thing that seemed reasonable at the time – he jumped feet-first into the booth.

Several employees – mostly teenage girls – were intently working on their assigned tasks when Mark made his surprise appearance.

Mark was nervous, so he spoke much faster than he normally would. "Can-I-hide-here-and-maybe-use-some-napkins-or-borrow-an-apron-for-a-while," Mark spewed as the candy bar workers, to Mark's horror, screamed bloody murder.

Mark instinctively lifted his hands up in front of him, as if to say, "No, no – I mean no harm," but by doing so, he exposed the genitals he had otherwise been covering. This led to more screaming.

Mark was about to take a step towards a pile of napkins. He figured if he could at least get that, maybe he could cover himself a little better. Then his foray into the candy bar booth wouldn't have been a total waste. But when he moved towards the napkins, the girl who had been coating the finished deep-fried product with powdered sugar shrieked. She flung an entire two-gallon size metal container of powdered sugar at him. Because his body was already wet from the rain, the powdered sugar covered his body.

Since the employees were backing away from him in terror, he decided there was little point in trying to explain himself and instead decided to make a swift exit. Mark leaped out of the booth just as quickly as he entered.

As the rain pelted him outside the booth, some of

the sugar began to dissipate. Mark actually found this disappointing since the sugar had done a nice job of covering his private areas. Looking at the surrounding booths, Mark tried to decide where to go next. He was about to head towards a cotton candy booth (*Great idea for underwear!* thought Mark) when he scratched at his chest. Mark felt a sudden burst of pain.

A bee was driving its stinger into Mark's chest. Mark angrily swatted it towards the ground. He was about to step on it when he felt the same pain burst into his neck. Then on his arm. Then his calf.

Mark looked all around, and just as he feared, they were everywhere. He was absolutely surrounded by bees.

Mark ran. He kept running as the bees chased him and as the rain drenched him and as the sugar dripped off of him. He had never felt so miserable.

Not knowing where to go, Mark made a quick decision. He saw a garbage truck driving through the middle of the road. Mark ran to the truck, climbed up the ladder on the side, and leapt inside. He buried himself in garbage, hoping the bees would lose track of him. It worked. He didn't feel any more stings. On the other hand, he was covered in garbage.

Finally feeling the privacy he was desperately craving since falling out of the Sky Ride, Mark decided to spend some quality time with the garbage for a while. He was in no hurry to get back out to the crowd. He really just needed to leave the fair altogether, but he was so unfamiliar with the layout. It seemed to go on forever.

The odor seeping from the bags of rotting food scraps was starting to get to Mark. He was more than a little nauseous and light-headed. Mark didn't think passing out in a garbage dumpster was the smartest idea, so he began pushing bags aside until he saw the sky again. Once he did, he leapt out of the garbage truck and ran to the nearest building.

Mark found himself surrounded by animals. Goats. Sheep. Pigs. And they all found Mark to be particularly interesting. Feeling that no good could come from spending any amount of time in this building, Mark turned to leave. As he did, he heard a voice say, "No, Bessie – git back here!"

A two-hundred pound hog was charging Mark. Coated in a sickly sweet mixture of sugar and garbage, Mark darted out of what he later discovered was the Miracle of Birth building and ran as fast as he could, the portly heffer following shortly behind him.

Mark booked it down Underwood Street, shoving people out of the way, his malodorous naked torso being quickly pursued by the beast. Mark kept glancing behind him, recognizing that the hog was gaining ground.

As Mark frantically ran towards the Grandstand – not out of purpose, just out of a lack of a coherent plan – he noticed something that triggered a memory. It was a food stand – Demitri's Gyros.

Then Mark saw another familiar sight. A red raincoat. It was Ashley.

She turned around just as Mark approached. "Mark..."

Mark grabbed her and shoved her to the ground, landing on top of her. The hog narrowly missed both of them and plunged into the siding of the Demitri's gyro stand. The food vendors were making a lot of commotion, but Mark focused on Ashley.

"Mark," she said. "You stink."

He lifted his naked body off of her. "Do you realize what I've been through?"

"Why are you still naked?" she asked."There's, like, a thousand t-shirts for sale."

Mark ground his teeth. "I've been chased, and grabbed, and caned, and sugared, and stung, and hunted– "

Ashley sighed. "Listen, I've had my gyro, my hair is getting wet – I think I'm just going to get going."

"But...you drove. Will you at least drive me home?"

"I would, but seriously Mark, I'm getting nauseous just being in your general vicinity. We should probably just go our separate ways."

"How will I get home?" asked Mark.

"There's literally like ten cops surrounding you right now," said Ashley.

Mark looked around. *Holy shit.*

"So, yeah..." said Ashley, standing up and fixing her clothes.

Mark began weeping as two uniformed officers, approaching from each side, tackled him and placed him in handcuffs.

"You really shouldn't be naked in public," said Ashley, as the cops led Mark away from the scene. "It's gross."

Untamed

Natalie Froman was at the zoo. Again.

It's not that she was bored of going to the Minnesota Zoo in her native Apple Valley; in fact, going to the zoo with her husband Steve and checking out the new exhibits was one of their favorite pastimes. With a continuously changing environment of new animals and new displays and attractions, the Minnesota Zoo kept Natalie and Steve quite busy in their early post-retirement years.

No, it wasn't the zoo that was bothering Natalie. It wasn't really Steve, either. It was the humdrum staleness of their relationship. Maybe it was just retirement in general that Natalie wasn't quite used to. Regardless, Natalie wanted something – anything – to spice up her life a little bit.

Which is why on this particular Thursday morning in late October, it took Natalie by as much surprise as Steve when she pulled him into a hidden enclave in the middle of the tropical bird sanctuary and proceeded to strip him of his clothes.

Fortunately, there were many little nooks and crannies throughout the tropical bird sanctuary, mostly for the explicit purpose of providing areas for students and nature lovers to get a closer look at the birds in more of a natural state.

For Natalie, it was an opportunity to see Steve in his natural state. Naked.

"What are you doing?" asked Steve, as Natalie pulled him into the hidden enclave.

"I just want to see something," said Natalie.

"Did you see a booby?" asked Steve, rubbing his short white beard with his free hand as Natalie yanked him with the other.

"Nope," said Natalie. *But you might,* she thought.

"A warbler? A titmouse?" asked Steve, scanning the lush jungle plantlife that covered and surrounded the faux cave structure. "What is it?"

Natalie pushed Steve against the cave. She kissed him on the lips.

"Are you okay?" he asked, looking confused.

"Yes, yes I'm fine," said Natalie. "I just...thought we could switch up the routine a little bit."

"But...we're at the zoo," said Steve, looking around nervously as Natalie continued to kiss him on the cheeks.

"What would be better?" whispered Natalie between kisses. "Costco? A highway rest stop? The zoo is just as good a place as any."

"I'm not sure about this," said Steve.

Natalie smiled. She could tell Steve's defenses were weakening.

Natalie kissed him on the lips. She wrapped her arms around his neck. "Let's make love," she said.

"But..." said Steve, "What if someone sees us? We're not the only guests here."

"That's part of the fun, silly."

A colorful, pointy-beaked bird streaked by Steve's head. He gulped.

"Honey," said Steve. "There are birds here. Really close to us."

"It's all part of the experience, sweetie. C'mon – just give it a chance."

Steve looked into his wife's eyes. He hadn't seen that lustful, pleading look in her eyes for a long time. Too long.

"Okay, Nat. You got it."

Steve and Natalie began to make out. Steve brushed his hand through Natalie's hair. Natalie clawed her hands down Steve's chest until she got to his belt buckle. They both lowered to their knees, and soon they were lying down. They moved from the enclave into the foliage itself.

"It's really hot in here," said Steve.

"It's the humidity," said Natalie. "There's only one solution. We have to take off your pants."

"I'm starting you think you have ulterior motives," said Steve.

"I'm not sure what you're referring to, mister." Natalie proceeded to remove Steve's pants and shirt. He was literally naked in the jungle.

"These leaves are surprisingly soft," said Steve, rubbing the leaves he was sitting on. "We should get some of these for the house."

"I'm getting jealous," said Natalie. "When are you going to strip me down?"

"How does right now sound?"

Natalie grinned from ear to ear as Steve stripped her clothes from her.

"I have a feeling we'll remember this for a very long time," said Natalie. She pressed her lips against Steves and continued to grind and thrust against him

It was the best sex Natalie had in years, and it wasn't simply due to the locale. The spontaneity, the thrill of getting caught, the rekindling of the excitement with her best friend and partner – it was amazing. In fact, she was about to reach what could have been one of the best orgasms of her life when, to her surprise and dismay, a voice interrupted.

"Excuse me."

Both Natalie and Steve stared at each other with horrified expressions.

"Excuse me, sir and ma'am?" The voice sounded friendly, not demanding.

Natalie turned her head to see a diminutive janitor with thick coke-bottle glasses holding a mop and pointing at them.

Steve also lifted his head to see who was speaking to them. He cleared his throat. "Umm...yes sir?"

"Sir and ma'am, I understand you may be hot due to the humidity and all, but zoo policy strictly forbids the removal of shirts and shoes on zoo grounds."

"Oh, I'm sorry," said Steve. "I didn't realize."

"Sir and ma'am, while wrestling is a healthy and

enjoyable pastime that I enjoy myself, it may not be appropriate in the dense jungle foliage."

Natalie was starting to think that the janitor may not be playing with a full deck.

"I understand," said Natalie, reaching for her clothes. "We didn't mean to hurt any of the plants."

"Oh, you won't hurt the plants," said the janitor. "They can protect themselves. Very poisonous. Not good for naked bodies."

Once again, Natalie and Steve exchanged horrified looks. Steve shifted Natalie's body off of his so he could move off of the incredibly comfortable green leaves he'd been enjoying. As he turned to pick up his pants, Natalie gasped.

"What is it?"

"Your back – it's completely red."

"Oh God," said Steve, and then shrugged. "It doesn't feel that bad, actually."

The janitor coughed. "In approximately thirty minutes, you will feel like you're being eaten alive by fire ants, yessir. One heck of a little plant, I tell you what."

Natalie looked confused. "Why would they put poisonous plants in a zoo?"

"As a purveyor of the custodial arts, I am not provided this information," said the janitor. "But my assumption is they were not counting on naked wrestling in an exhibit meant for birds, not humans."

"That makes sense," said Natalie.

"That's just a guess, though," said the janitor. "Please don't quote me on any of these matters."

"Why would – OW!" yelled Steve, swatting at his

back. "WHAT THE – "

"What was that?" asked Natalie, concerned. She saw something flap away from Steve.

"Something bit me," said Steve. "Like, really, really bit me. Son of a..."

"Sir and ma'am, I do believe that was a South African Rosashirp. It attacks things that are red in color. Boy, now that I think about it, that sure is an unfortunate combination with your back rashes, I tell you what."

Another bird dive-bombed Steve. He scrambled to his feet, reaching for his clothes. As he was about to put on his pants, he heard a screeching caw right next to his ear. Steve panicked. He threw his clothes aside and ran.

"Steve?" called Natalie, holding her shirt against her bare chest. "Steve, where the heck are you running to?

"Ma'am, I do believe your husband took exception to the birds plunging their beaks into his backside." The janitor pushed the bridge of his coke-bottle glasses back up his nose.

Natalie grimaced as she put her pants back on. "I know that," she said. "I just don't know where he thinks he's going to. I mean, what is he going to find down that passage?"

"Well, ma'am," said the janitor, "that largely depends on which direction he goes. If he takes a left, he will be in our café, just past the restrooms."

"Okay," said Natalie. "What if he takes a right?"

"That would be the baboon sanctuary."

Natalie's eyes grew wide.

"Ma'am, you have a funny look on your face."

"STEVE!" Natalie yelled as she too ran down the

hallway where just seconds ago her husband had fled butt-naked from some angry aviaries.

"Ma'am, would you like me to...? I'll just follow you, then. Yup. That's what I'll do."

***

Natalie pulled her shirt over her head and she turned the corner to the baboon sanctuary.

"Steve? Steve, where are you?" she called out as she searched hallway. There were a fair number of guests, but Natalie figured her husband would stand out, what with being completely nude.

A familiar voice behind her said, "Excuse me, ma'am?"

Natalie rolled her eyes. She turned around.

"Yes?"

"Ma'am, are you looking for your husband?"

Natalie, without much forethought or control, gave the lowly janitor a nasty, disapproving look.

"Yes, yes I'm looking for my husband. He was the one that just got attacked by birds. Remember? It was thirty seconds ago."

The janitor shrugged. "I assumed that was the case. Anyhow, ma'am, you may wish to contact your husband, as he is currently directly to your left."

Natalie turned to her left, then turned back to the janitor.

"There's no one there," she said.

"Ma'am, it would be advisable to look further. In particular, about twenty yards past the plexiglass."

"Past the..."

Natalie's jaw dropped. She saw her husband. Her dear, sweet husband, who less than an hour ago was resistant to the idea of taking off his clothes in a zoo. He was running, his hands behind his back, scratching at red, itchy flesh. To make matters worse, he was being very closely chased by an overly-aroused baboon. It seemed to be hypnotized by Steve's red backside.

This would probably be the last time he took any of her suggestions for spicing up their love life.

"Ma'am, would you like me to call security?"

"Yes, yes call now. This should not be happening."

"They've gotten awfully close. It looks like they're wrestling, too. Just like you guys were!"

Natalie let out a sigh of unbelievable sadness. "Call security. Please."

***

Natalie and Steve sat on uncomfortable, stiff metal chairs. Florescent lights flickered and zapped overhead. A security officer kept tapping his pen against his clipboard. *Tap.Tap.Tap.Tap.*

"Tell me again how everyone's clothes seemed to disappear?"

Steve was wearing a generic volunteer shirt and a pair of workpants provided by the zoo, since his other clothes were still covered with poisonous pollens from the bird sanctuary.

"It's not like that —" Steve began to say, but the security officer shushed him up.

"No, nothing from you," said the officer. "Not yet."

Steve was offended, but knew better than to talk back to authority. Besides, he didn't have much wind left in his sails.

"Sherman, can you tell me what happened?" asked the security officer.

The janitor took his glasses off, wiped them with a rag in his back pocket, then put them on again. "Yes, sir, I would be most obliged. When I came across the guests in our bird sanctuary, I saw them wrestling naked. At first I didn't think much of it, because I've seen a lot of the prairie dogs and even the gazelle doing the same thing in their exhibits. Never seen guests do that before, no sir. That was unexpected."

"Sherman, you say they were...wrestling naked?" The security officer looked at Steve and Natalie with a smirk on his face.

Steve and Natalie's faces grew bright red.

"Yes, sir. Quite naked."

"Who was winning?"

Sherman rubbed his chin. "Well, sir – I'm certainly no wrestling official. She spent a significant amount of time on top of him, which leads me to believe that she would be deemed the winner."

The security officer nodded with amusement.

Natalie lowered her head and covered her eyes.

"Although I think she tried using some kind of bridge hold on him," said the janitor, "because her head was below his belt for a long –"

"OKAY," yelled Steve. "I think that's quite enough. Are you going to call the real police and have us arrested, or can we go?"

"Just one more question," said the security officer. "I totally understand the poisonous foliage you were lying on and how that resulted in the South African Rosashirps attacking you.

But when you tried to run away, why did you jump into the baboon sanctuary?"

Steve thought for a moment. "Honestly, I was more concerned with people seeing me naked in the hallway, so I wanted to duck away somewhere I wouldn't be seen."

"Then the baboon saw you."

"Right," said Steve, "but comparatively speaking, I felt a little more dominant, so I figured I'd be fine."

The security officer laughed as he crossed his arms. "Those baboons are heading into mating season, and we've been supplying them with enough hormone to make sure it happens."

Steve stared at him. "Well, I know that *now*, obviously."

Natalie patted her husband on the leg.

"Let's go home, honey," she said.

"We sure hope you enjoyed your time at the Minnesota Zoo, folks," said Sherman. "Please come back soon!"

"...but not too soon," said the security officer, winking.

A Ski Lift Named Desire

Karen was not an experienced skier by any means, but she did appreciate an excuse to take a Friday off work and spend a long weekend with her boyfriend Kent. She had a stressful job as a paralegal in downtown Minneapolis, working for condescending a-holes that she'd prefer to avoid in her after-hours, non-work life. Kent was the opposite of the attorney partners that ran the firm. He was down to earth. He was kind. He had a sparse bank account, but was generous with what he had.

He was also very late. When Karen arrived at Wild Mountain, she thought Kent would be waiting for her. Instead, she got a text from him saying that he was held up at work, but he was expecting to be there soon.

Just happy to be away from work, Karen entered the ski resort's lodge. She went to the bar and ordered a whiskey.

"You sure you can handle that?" asked the bartender.

"Don't worry – I'm a pro," said Karen. "Besides, it's

been a long week. I could use it."

"Fair enough," said the bartender, smiling. "Just don't go skiing into any trees now. We don't need a Sonny Bono situation on our hands."

"No guarantees," said Karen. "Just keep the liquor coming until I tell you to stop."

"Whatever you say."

Karen liked hearing that for once. Usually it was the other way around.

After her first glass of whiskey disappeared, Karen looked at her watch. Where was he? Kent wasn't the type to let work take precedence over her.

"Pour me another?" asked Karen.

"Sure thing," said the bartender. "Do me a favor though? Try not to turn our white snow into a nasty beige color."

"I don't get sick," said Karen.

"That's what they all say."

Karen took another sip. Then she heard her phone buzz. Kent had texted her. It said:

Be there in ten. Hope you're ready to see me!

Karen tipped her glass back. She was already anxious that she had to wait so long. Now that she had a little alcohol in her system, she was craving him even more. She thought about pushing him into the woods and jumping on top of him. Or maybe they could find a little private area behind the chalet? At any rate, she wanted to have a little more fun than just an average day of going down the slopes.

"Excuse me, but are you okay?" asked the bartender.

"Muff better," said Karen.

"Pardon?"

"Umm good. I'm tozally good."

"Here's your bill. Pay whenever you're ready."

Karen used her sad puppy dog face. "Can't I haff one more?"

"I'm afraid not," said the bartender. "Have a good evening. And I'd suggest waiting a good long while before even considering the bunny hills."

Karen scowled, but remained silent. She laid her head on the bar for just a moment...or maybe it was several minutes? At any rate, she was stirred awake by the tapping of a finger on her shoulder.

"What the f—" Karen began to say. Then she saw him. "Kent!"

He was standing next to her. She was surprised to see that he was already in his ski gear. Did he have time to get there and change all before waking her up? How long was she out? Kent looked down at her with concern.

"Karen, have you been drinking?"

"No," she said. "I mean, not much. A little, obviously. I am at a bar."

"Why didn't you hit the slopes? You could have skied while you waited for me."

Karen shrugged. "Well, sure I could have. But I wanted to do this."

"Karen," said Kent as he shook his head, "you know I don't like it when you drink. You get...weird. I've been trying to get you sober for two years."

Karen made a duck face. "I never get to have any fun."

Kent sighed. "Are you still up for this?"

"Of course, baby," said Karen, smiling. "Let's get it on."

"Behave yourself now," said Kent.

Karen slapped him on the chest. "We'll see about that."

***

Karen and Kent stood at the foot of the snow hills. Karen was about to push off towards the ski lift when she wobbled off balance and had to grab Kent by the shoulder.

"You're absolutely sure you're up for this?"

"Yes, definitely," said Karen, rebalancing herself.

Kent kissed her on the cheek. She enjoyed the brief warmth it provided. It also sparked something in her. Something that sent shivers through the rest of her body. It made her...antsy.

"Let's get going," said Karen. "Last one to the ski lift is a rotten egg." She used the ski poles to thrust herself in the direction of the ski lift. Kent was in close pursuit.

"Oh, no you don't," said Kent, as Karen was about to reach the ski lift first. He neared her, caught her by the back of the jacket, and pulled her towards him.

"What do you think you're doing, mister?"

Kent wrapped his arms around her. "Sorry I got mad earlier," he said. "I love you."

"I love you too," said Karen.

On the weekends, there was usually a line of skiers and snowboards waiting to get on the ski lift. Karen was happy to see that on this particular Friday, there was no line to speak of. They were able to approach and jump on the next available chair.

Karen saw that Kent was paying extra close attention to making sure that she got on the ski lift properly and wasn't about to fall out on her slightly intoxicated ass. She didn't like being in need of someone else's care, but it still made her happy that Kent thought of her.

"Not too many people out here," said Kent.

"Most people are still at work," said Karen, grabbing his leg. Kent looked down at her hand.

"Say, what are you doing there?"

Karen rubbed his thigh, working her way up north. "What do you think?"

Kent's face grew bright red. "Karen, we're not the only ones here. It's daytime. People can see us."

"It's overcast at best," said Karen. "Besides, no one will be looking at us...THIS closely." She gently squeezed his balls.

"WHA!" shrieked Kent in an unusually high octave for him.

"What was that?" asked Karen.

Kent coughed. "What do you say to just some light kissing, sweetie?"

Karen rolled her eyes. "Really, Kent? You think I want a peck on the cheek like a thirteen-year-old?"

Karen returned her hands from Kent's pants to her own.

"What are you doing?" asked Kent, nervous.

"Getting this party started," said Karen, as she

unbuckled her belt.

"Stop," said Kent as he searched back and forth for on-lookers.

"Too late," said Karen, yanking down her pants. "My lotion is in motion. Let's get this going."

Kent scrunched his eyes and shook his head. "This is why I wish you wouldn't drink. It always leads to trouble."

Karen froze.

Kent gulped.

"Really, Kent?"

"I'm just saying –"

"What are you saying Kent? That I'm an annoying alcoholic? That you don't like being with me?"

"I didn't say – "

"You didn't have to Kent. It's so damned obvious. A couple years ago you would have jumped at the possibility of fucking me on a ski lift."

"Highly unlikely..." muttered Kent.

"I just wanted one little moment of excitement," said Karen, attempting to pull up her pants and underwear. She was surprised to find she was having some trouble.

"I'm sorry," said Kent. "I suppose our lives have grown somewhat dull."

"Uh-huh," said Karen, vigorously yanking at her jeans.

"I mean, yes – the drinking does bother me, but I know it's a lot better than it was. Perhaps I should be more understanding."

"Yup, understanding," said Karen, looking down

between her legs.

"To be honest, I sort of feel like a schmuck for neglecting you. If I wasn't so busy at work all the time and was able to give you more attention, maybe you wouldn't turn to things like alcohol..."

"Yeah, honey – we have a problem," said Karen, panicked.

"Yes, we can call it 'our' problem. I think that's good. We should both take ownership," said Kent, patting Karen on the back.

"No, Kent. I'm saying we have a real fucking problem. Shit –"

"What's going on?"

Karen groaned. "You know how in *A Christmas Story* how little Ralphie gets his tongue stuck to the flag pole?"

"Yeah?"

"Well, the same thing happened."

"What are you talking about?"

"Goddammit. My vagina is frozen to the seat."

Kent almost fell off the ski lift from surprise, and then from leaning too far forward to get a better look.

"So...what do we do?" asked Kent.

"Fuck if I know," said Karen. "I've never had this happen before. This isn't one of those things that people warn you about."

"Well, how many people would try to apply their bare nethers to a ski lift?"

"Seriously, Kent – do you think that's helping right now?

Kent sighed. "I suppose not. What do we do?"

"Don't you think I'm trying to figure that out?"

"Fine, fine," said Kent. "Just stop yelling."

"Okay," said Karen.

"I've got an idea," said Kent. "We just need to warm it up, right? Let me just try rubbing it a bit – "

Kent thrust out his hand towards Karen's troubled private area.

"Here, how does this feel – "

"Ow, ow, ow – no, no. Stop."

"What?"

Karen grinded her teeth. "It's very sore down there, as you can imagine."

"Oh, sure," said Kent.

"Any other ideas?"

"Yeah...it's gross though."

"I really don't care at this point. What is it?"

"Well, I could try to loosen it up by...you know...blowing warm air at it, I guess."

Karen wrinkled her nose. "What?"

"Well, it probably just needs some warm moisture. So I suppose I could spit on it. I mean, unless you want me peeing on you."

"Good God, stop it."

"Just an idea."

Karen closed her eyes. "Okay, fine – just blow on it a bit. Let's see if it works."

Kent nodded. He leaned forward, trying to get a good angle. As he did so, his butt slipped from the chair and he fell, flinging his arms out at the last moment to catch the edge of the seat. "

"Oh my God," said Karen.

"Help me!" yelled Kent, barely keeping grip on the

edge of the seat.

Karen grabbed him by the arms and yanked. As she did so, she was also pulling herself forward on the chair. Karen screamed.

Kent was able to get enough grip on Karen and the chair to hoist himself back up onto the seat.

"That was scary," said Kent.

"That was painful," said Karen.

"Are you loose?" asked Kent, looking in the direction of Karen's nether region.

"No, I don't think so – it just hurts worse."

Kent rubbed Karen's thigh. "I'm sorry, sweetie."

Karen choked back a sob. "I feel so stupid."

"Hey," said Kent, bringing his palm up to her cheek. "You're not stupid. I'm the stupid one. I've been neglecting you to the point where you wanted to do something crazy."

"It's not your fault," sniffed Karen. "I shouldn't have had so much to drink. If I was sober, I probably would have kept my pants on."

"Shh," said Kent, stroking her hair. "it will be okay."

Kent lifted her chin and kissed her on the lips. The kiss developed into a powerful make-out session that continued significantly longer than Kent had expected. He was about to pull away when Karen wrapped her arms around him and pulled him in closer.

"Karen, I – "

"Don't stop."

Karen held Kent tight as he continued to kiss her. She was passionate, insatiable. He could feel her heart beat against his.

"I love you," he whispered in between smooches.

"I love you, too," she said, her body squirming against his.

Squirming...?

"Oh my God, I'm free!" exclaimed Karen.

"...but how?"

Karen laughed. "Apparently I got just excited enough."

"Huh," said Kent, shaking his head. "Biology is weird."

Within seconds, Karen had her pants pulled up, covering her aching, sore undercarriage.

"You'll be okay?" asked Kent.

"I think so. Would you be terribly offended if I wanted a glass of wine before we leave?"

"I don't blame you one bit," said Kent. "And I'll be happy to join you."

"Let's get down from here," said Karen. "And never come back."

"Whatever you want, sweetheart."

Fifty Shades of Grand Marais

The North Star Lodge along Lake Superior's northern tip was vast and serene. Most of its thousands of annual visitors would describe it as picturesque. Perhaps even wondrous or heavenly. In the winter months, however, the owner and proprietor felt quite differently. While he certainly couldn't disregard or deny the natural beauty of Grand Marais, Dougie St. Beige found the great white north to be completely and utterly *boring.*

A man of peculiar tendencies, Beige spent his substantial free time constructing miniature outhouses for the lodge's plentiful squirrel population. While he did spend some lonely evenings attempting to lure said squirrels into using the outhouses, he typically grew depressed when they failed to do so. On those occasions, he assumed he had yet to construct the ultimate outhouse, so he would go back to work, carving out little wood johns perfectly contoured to the furry backends of his little friends.

From November to April, he had few guests other than hunters and fishermen to occupy the dozens of rooms at the lodge. Most of them were too busy with their sport to even notice Beige's hobby. That didn't bother him one bit. He wasn't doing it to get attention. He simply wanted to fill hours between maintaining the property and checking-in guests.

Beige's mother, who had passed on the lodge to her son after the death of her husband so she could concentrate her efforts on drinking martinis in the Florida Keys, had been keeping a close eye on the condition of not only the lodge, but also her son.

"You need help," she had told him last November.

"I know. This is way too much lodge for one man to take care of," said Beige.

"That's not what I meant, Dougie. It's true, the condition of the lodge is deteriorating. Sure, it's getting old. That tends to happen. But I can tell you're not spending much time clearing out cobwebs and repainting walls. Honestly, what do you spend all of your time doing?"

Dougie St. Beige shrugged. "Little of this, little of that."

"Why are there dozens of little wood boxes outside along the shore?"

"They're not boxes, they're –"

"Don't tell me, Dougie – I know there's no acceptable answer to that question, so let's just let it go."

"Okay, Mom."

"Dougie, I've taken the liberty of hiring an assistant for you. I don't want this lodge to fall into disarray. It's yours now, but I will not stand to see it crumble to the ground. Megan will be starting on Monday. She'll be doing most of the cleaning around the lodge so you can concentrate on maintenance. And I do mean maintenance – *not* building...whatever those things are."

"Mom, I don't want anyone else here. I like my privacy. I like having this place to myself."

"This is a lodge. You cater to guests. You should *want* people to come here."

Beige shrugged.

"Listen, Dougie – just be nice to Megan. She's your employee, so utilize her. Tell her what you want her to do. Do you think you can handle that?"

"Sure, I guess."

Dougie's mom opened her purse and withdrew a cigarette and a lighter. She lit the cigarette and took a deep drag.

"I have a five o'clock flight back to Florida. If you have any issues around here, call me. And for God's sake, Dougie – take a shower."

Dougie sniffed his armpits. He scrunched his nose.

"I love you, Dougie," said his mom. Within a couple hours, she was on her way to the airport, leaving Dougie in blissful peace and quiet.

***

On Monday morning, Dougie St. Beige awoke to the sound of boisterous knocking. He was surprised – only one person knew which room was his, and she was likely eating an early bird breakfast at a beach café right now. Not to mention that no one other than his mother knew that his room existed; after all, the only way to access his room was to pull a cord hanging from the ceiling near the utilities room. Many years ago, his father had insisted that Dougie make his room in the attic as to not occupy a room that could otherwise be generating cash. As more lodges were built in the area and demand for rooms decreased, Dougie decided that he preferred his private space and continued to live there.

And his space was just that – *private*. Which made him very surprised to hear knocking.

"Hello?" he called out, wiping the sleep out of his eyes.

The knocking persisted.

"Who's there?"

Dougie rolled out of bed and stood up, then jumped when he realized the wooden boards that made up his floor were freezing cold. He proceeded to put on his bunny slippers as he meandered towards the floor entrance.

"You need to pull the cord," Dougie yelled down through the floor.

The square panel lowered and a ladder descended. Dougie could only see a dress from his vantage point.

"Who's there?" he asked.

"My name is Megan," a voice said. "Ms. St. Beige hired me to help you with the lodge. Shall I come up there, or...?"

Dougie looked around the attic. One of the advantages of having a private location is not having to worry about anyone actually seeing it. Dougie had a plethora of dirty articles of clothing strewn about haphazardly. In addition, he had an impressively large collection of magazines ranging from *National Geographic* to *Hairy Hunnies*. Dougie decided it might be best if he head downstairs.

"I'll be right down, Megan. Give me a minute."

"Okay, Mr. St. Beige," said the voice from downstairs.

Dougie wrapped himself in a robe, although he left it relatively loose. He wanted to ensure that this young woman could get a glance at his bits and pieces as he crawled down the ladder.

"Ready or not, here I come," yelled Dougie as he descended the ladder one rung at a time.

As Dougie jumped from the ladder to the floor, he was awestruck by the most beautiful woman with a horrified look on her face. Dougie liked that sort of thing.

"Mr. St. Beige, you should really consider putting on some clothes," said Megan, directing her eyes in the opposite direction of her new boss.

"I think not," said Dougie. "This is my home. I like to be comfortable."

"Mr. St. Beige, your dear sweet mother hired me to work for you. I would appreciate it if you would at least attempt to be decent during the daylight hours. However...umm, *comfortable* you choose to be at night is up to you."

Megan crossed her arms across her chest.

Dougie looked her up and down. "So you're my new assistant? That means I can fire you. You have to do whatever I say."

"That's not how it works," said Megan.

"I'm pretty sure I can fire you."

"I'm not going anywhere. Your mom will keep paying me."

"But you still have to do what I say," said Dougie.

"Within reason," said Megan.

"Will you clean all the restrooms in the guest suites?"

"With the low occupancy, that shouldn't be a problem," said Megan.

"Will you clean the outhouses?"

"Probably not."

"You don't like outhouses?" asked Dougie. He thought of his custom-made squirrel outhouses.

"Not particularly," said Megan.

Dougie frowned. "Why are you here?"

"Your mom doesn't want to see her family's business go into ruins. I'm here to help you maintain the property and keep the business thriving."

"Will you take your clothes off?"

"No."

"Will you wear a French maid outfit?"

"No."

"Can I..." Dougie began to say as he untied the belt on his robe.

"MR. ST. BEIGE!

"Just kidding," he said as re-tightened the robe's belt.

Megan grimaced. "I don't think you are, which is what disturbs me."

Dougie shrugged.

"Listen, I will do what I can to help out around here and keep you focused on what matters. I'm talking about renovation projects, bookkeeping, maintenance...not doing God knows what in the attic. And no more sexually suggestive comments. Got it?"

"I don't think I like you anymore," said Dougie.

"Tough. Because you're stuck with me."

Dougie uttered a *humph* and ascended the ladder to his humble abode.

***

At 9:00 the next morning, Dougie St. Beige awoke to the sound of a truck honking its horn. Dougie got excited since he was pretty sure he knew what it was. He hopped down through the attic door, skipping the ladder altogether. He ran towards the lobby. When he arrived, he discovered that Megan was already there. She was dressed in a pair of jeans and a plaid checkered shirt. Next to her was the UPS delivery man with a tall box beside him. Megan was signing for his package.

Megan waved goodbye to the delivery man and began carrying the tall box.

"Whoa, whoa – hold on, that's my package," said Dougie.

"Good morning, Mr. St. Beige."

"Good morning to you, too. But seriously, that's my package. I want it."

"It was delivered here, addressed to the lodge," said Megan. "Was it ordered for the lodge or is it something of a personal nature?"

"Personal," said Dougie.

"Okay. But it's addressed to the lodge. Did you use your own funds or did you charge this to the lodge?"

Dougie grinded his teeth. "I don't think you should work here anymore."

"Too bad. Shall we open this box?"

"No."

"I think we should."

"That's a bad idea."

Megan looked frightened."Why?"

"It would confuse you."

"Let's find out," said Megan. She rummaged through the drawers of the lobby desk until she found a box   cutter.

"Hey, you can't do this," said Dougie. "This is an invasion of my privacy."

"Not at all," said Megan. "Whatever is in this box is lodge property. As an employee of North Star Lodge, I have every right to open this box." Megan looked at Dougie directly. "If you want privacy, start using your own money for personal items."

Dougie gritted his teeth."Fine."

Megan smiled. "Good." She used the box cutter to cut open the top part of the box. She lifted the top. "Oh my."

"It's not that strange," said Dougie.

Megan lifted objects out of the box. "How many of them are there?"

"A few."

"More like a dozen it looks like," said Megan, lifting

one after another out of the box. "What do you possibly need with all of these?"

"I can explain."

"I mean, really!" said Megan. "What does one man need with a dozen taxidermied squirrels?"

"It's for a project I've been working on," said Dougie.

"Project?"

"Yes, a very important project."

"Explain," said Megan.

"Well, you see, I...umm..."

"Yes?"

"Maybe it's better if I show you."

"Okay," she said."Show me."

Dougie St. Beige led her through the lobby, down the guestroom hall, and through the backdoors towards the patio. It had been cold overnight, and a light snow coated almost everything outside.

"What are all those boxes?" asked Megan.

"That's my project."

Megan looked confused.

"Your project is a bunch of wooden boxes?"

"No, no...nothing that dull. Come – take a look."

Dougie led her to the first box that lay just beyond the patio, just prior to the entrance of a nature trail that meandered through the lodge's property.

"Did you carve this yourself?" asked Megan.

"Oh, yes. Every little crevice. This...this is my life's work."

"A wooden box?"

"No! You're missing it. Look closer." Dougie wiped

a layer of snow that had accumulated inside the box.

"Oh, so you carved a teeny little chair inside the box. And it has a hole in it."

"Keep looking," said Dougie.

"Is that...a tiny roll of toilet paper?"

Dougie grinned from ear to ear. "Yes! I used a paper shredder to cut toilet paper thin enough. Then I rolled it onto a thimble and installed it. Oh, and here's the best part – the hole in the toilet goes straight through the bottom. You can literally pick up and move the box when the hole gets full. No clean up!"

Megan looked around her. There was a row of boxes lined up, seemingly going all the way through the nature trail. She looked back at Dougie St. Beige, who was wide-eyed and excited.

"Dougie – who is going to use these...outhouses?"

"Well, who do you think, silly? The squirrels!"

"Why would squirrels need outhouses?"

Dougie blinked. "Would you want to go to the bathroom outside? Exposed?"

"I'm pretty sure the squirrels are used to it."

Dougie shook his head. "No, this is changing every-thing. This is sophisticating nature. Our creature friends don't have to be just animals anymore. This is evolution happening – right before your very eyes!"

Megan swallowed. "Have any squirrels actually, you know, used the outhouses?"

"Well, no, not yet. These things don't happen overnight. I've tried my best to lead them into the outhouses and show them how to use it, but so far they haven't responded. These things take a long time. I have no doubt it could be years before my project is complete."

"Your project? You mean when all the squirrels begin using your outhouses?"

Dougie nodded. "Exactly."

"Why did you order one dozen stuffed squirrels?"

"That's a fair question. Since my little friends haven't proactively used the outhouses, I thought it might help them to see them in use. That's why you'll find that all the squirrels I ordered were custom-stuffed in the sitting position."

"Custom stuffed?"

"Yeah, taxidermy. It's quite an art."

"Dougie... why would – "

"I believe I'm your boss. Please call me Mr. St. Beige."

"Sure, right. Mr. St. Beige. If you were a squirrel, would seeing the dead carcass of one of your friends inspire you to try new things?"

Dougie crossed his arms. He rubbed his chin. He was pensive. "That's a deep question. I'm not quite sure how to respond to that."

"Let me try a simpler question. How many hours per week do you typically spend on this project?"

"Approximately thirty hours a week," said Dougie.

"How many hours do you take care of the lodge?"

"Approximately twelve hours a week."

"Don't you think that's a little lopsided?"

Dougie smirked. "I love what I do," he said. "Specifically the squirrel stuff and not-so-much the lodge stuff."

"Okay – well, thank you for showing me all this," said Megan.

Dougie held out his hand. "The pleasure was all mine. You know, I can already tell that you really get what I'm trying to do here. That's just so cool."

"Yeah, definitely," said Megan. "Keep up the good work. I'm going to go now."

"Back to the grindstone – I love it. Listen, Megan – I wasn't sure about you at first, but I'm feeling pretty good about this whole thing. Me and you are going to get along real well."

"Yes, right," said Megan.

"Sorry about that joke about wearing a French maid outfit earlier. I was just joshing around. You know how us guys are."

"I'm going now."

"Right. Well, take it easy! Keep truckin'!" Dougie held his thumb up and Megan walked speedily back through the patio door and into the lobby.

***

During midday, Megan quietly snuck into the lobby office. She could hear a buzz saw going, so she figured she could have a phone conversation without being overheard by Dougie. She had tried to use her cell phone, but reception was just impossible. Megan pulled a folded piece of paper out of her jeans pocket. It had a phone number written on it. She picked up the landline phone and called.

She heard an answer on the other end.

"Hello?"

"Ms. St. Beige. It's me. Megan."

"Oh, dear – how are you enjoying the lodge? Don't you just love it?"

"I do, Margaret – it's beautiful. Actually, it's exactly what I'm looking for. I'm so glad you mentioned to my father that you were looking to sell it."

"Me and your father go way back, dear – but enough of that saucy history. I hope you've been delicate on my poor Dougie."

"I think I've been nice as possible. I introduced myself as a helper, just like you wanted. One thing I don't understand, though. He really seems to think he owns the place."

Megan heard a sigh.

"A couple years ago after Dougie's father passed away, I tried to transfer the property into Dougie's name. I thought he was old enough to handle the responsibility. But Dougie has always been...different. I knew there was a problem when I asked him to sign the deed, and instead of signing his name, he drew little paw prints."

"Wow. So you still own the property?"

"Yes, I most certainly do."

"And you're willing to sell it?"

"Yes, at a very reasonable price. But it comes with a condition."

"Oh no," said Megan.

"Oh yes. If you buy the property, you must continue to employ Dougie. I want to make sure he has a roof over his head."

"Does he still have to live in the lodge? I don't know

if I can live with that."

Silence.

"That's up to you. Help him find nearby lodging. Watch out for him."

"Okay. I'll take it."

"The lodge? You want to buy?"

"Yes, it's beautiful! I love it!"

"Wonderful! I'll send over the contract this evening. But please remember – go easy on Dougie. He's a sweet boy."

"Of course."

***

At 8:30pm, Dougie was sitting on the edge of his bed in the attic. He had four stuffed squirrels sitting on little pillows on the floor.

"So, I guess what I'm trying to say, guys, is I really think she, like, *gets me.* You know?"

Dougie scratched his head. Sawdust fell out of his hair from when he had been constructing new outhouse boxes earlier in the day.

"C'mon, Carlos – don't tell me you've never thought about girls before. Caaaarlos. You can be honest here, buddy."

Once again, Carlos the Squirrel was giving him the silent treatment.

"I just hope that I can find the kind of love that Bonnie and Nester found. Right guys?"

Dougie pushed two of the squirrels closer together, but one of them fell off its pillow and tumbled head-first to the wood boards that made up the floor. "Oh, gosh – sorry Nester. That was definitely my fault. Thank God Rico is a doctor." Dougie reached onto his nightstand and grabbed a tissue. He draped it around Rico's frame. Dougie thought Rico looked just like Dr. Finkel, his pediatrician growing up. "Gosh, Rico – are you some kind of impersonator?"

He was about to delve into the careers and life stories of Bonnie and Nester, but his playtime was disturbed by a loud knocking on the floor of the attic.

Dougie got excited. "This is it, guys! She wants to see me! High fives!" Dougie proceeded to give each of the squirrels a high five, as promised.

The knocking grew louder.

"I'm coming, I'm coming."

Dougie shoved down the attic door, which caused the ladder to slide down. He walked down, one step at a time. He was expecting to see Megan, but there was no one in sight. But he did notice a yellow slip of paper taped to the attic door.

Dougie picked it up and read it. It was an Eviction Notice.

"Nuts," he said.

Acknowledgments

Writing this book would not have been possible without the incredible support of my wife Michelle. She either told me, "That's hilarious!" or "That's disgusting – don't do that" in all the right places. She also added a lot of inspiration...*if you know what I mean!* But I'm not supposed to talk about that.

Many thanks to my best friend Andy Pogreba, who not only provided the idea for the glorious twine ball story during a night of excessive drinking, but also continued to give me plenty of encouragement along the way.

As always, thank you to Jessie Chandler for providing feedback, advice, encouragement, and lots of hugs. What an amazing person.

Thank you to my parents for being supportive, despite the topic and theme of the stories. That's what makes you cool parents.

Thank you to all the bookstores for supporting me the last several years. It's meant so much to me!

Most importantly, thank YOU – the reader – for trying something new and going on this ride with me